DOES *Love* REALLY BITE???

LAKSHMI C RADHAKRISHNAN

PARTRIDGE
A Penguin Random House Company

To order additional copies of this book, contact
Partridge India
000 800 10062 62
www.partridgepublishing.com/india
orders.india@partridgepublishing.com

CONTENTS

PROLOGUE

To me, it has been quite an adventurous ride towards being an author. But the immense love and support from my readers have kept my spirit live which in turn has resulted in getting this novel published.

Once again, it's the almighty and my family I owe to for supporting me to work towards my passion with much peace and the blessings of my father who has left for heavenly abode. If not his motivation, I see myself in some other portal leaving arts and literature.

I'm thankful to Ms. Gemma Ramos, my Publishing Services Associate of Partridge Publishing India who has patiently tolerated my unending queries and lack of technical know how by constantly guiding me through my work as an author.

My first venture 'Colours Of Life' and the second innings 'My Book Of Love' had been a collection of emotions portrayed through characters that would be familiar to you by now. This time, 'Does love really bite???" is sure to be a part of your life as Akruti tries to define love in different dimensions forced by the circumstances she has to live with.

This you may call it a fiction or non-fiction owing to the thin line of difference as this has happened to each of us. If not completely at least a minute part of it.

I believe it is your life as well because some time, some where, some one would have definitely forced you to think . . .
Does love really bite???

Wish you a pleasant journey through Akruti's life!!

Lakshmi C Radhakrishnan

CHAPTER 1

The big day

The Windsor Chapel thronged with guests. All male folk, black and groomed swarmed like bees mumbling in harmony. And to their opposite, the congress of angels with white washed faces and gleaming smiles kept their hands busy in touch-ups. The air was whipped with fragrance of fresh cologne blended with rich perfume giving it mushy aura.

In couple of minutes, the chapel turned alive and the orchestra broke the grave silence that had lingered. From the right end a tall knight like figure appeared. Though not in armor, his tux held tight to his well built physique. With shiny eyes he stood absolutely still. His face was pale with little or no emotions at all. At count of ten, the bride appeared; a swan all white floating towards him in rhythm. Her long yet heavily brocaded veil followed her but at a distance. The satin figure held his hand once she had neared him. The vows began. It was the grooms turn . . . . and he stood still. His silence sounded louder than the screams of agony. Yet he stood unperturbed. His eyes spoke. When they met hers, she sighed and in a minute she tightened the grip of his palm and turned it to a handshake.

"Leave if you will. I wish you all good. You can't be happy with me. With so much love that still remains in you, you have to leave. I will make my life. I always did and will. So, please before my mind turns evil, leave for good!"

He looked at her for one last time and kissed her palm. She felt them moisten with his tears. He left silently leaving the spectators echo into murmur that grew louder at each step he took towards the exit. Now the exit was his gateway to freedom. He meant no harm to the lady he had abandoned at the chapel. She was kind, a gem at heart and full of love, the love that could even bear shame to let him live. Ricky would live and live his own life.

All he wanted was a full life and a life full of love he yearned for. Destiny had stored misery and a deserted life for his fate. Hopes were cursed and tears were blessed in bounty. His scarred face was his only belonging. Whatever he had earned turned into sand, so was the boon. Everything flowed through his fingers against his will. He had nothing but prayers and tears to offer; for even that would seem meager for a life he dreamt.

I, me, myself—Akruti

"I admit, I shouldn't have been so rude but she forced me to. She wanted to convert my mom into a fashion bug cum brand freak. That's two in one and too much to ask for. The taunt for using cheap market goods as she says and the show off ramp performance filled with high degree vanity and shrewdness could have been avoided." She murmured in disgust.

This happened every year. The ritual had been on for more than 3 years and has added colors and flavors after the Raizadas have met Rais 3 years back . . .

3 years is enough to forget any mishap that hurt but for her, this ritual created fresh wounds that have left scars from within.

*   *   *

The phone echoed. A least expected one. Shishirji apologized for what happened during the day. Shishir ji . . . that's what I called his dad. He did persuade to make me call him 'Uncle' but Mrs. Mrinali's ego and the respect she held in her friends' circle just deprived me the right to call her Aunty. Sruthy, Rahul's only sister, an angel at heart with a pale face and pink cheeks had been doing her graduation course when I met her for the first time. Sending me gifts were her hobby, followed by complaints for not writing to her.

She'd a mobile phone at this age . . . Don't you think it's too early? Well, I did. But that was yet another life pattern of the Raizadas. You wouldn't believe what Rahul got for his 18th year of life on earth . . . a Ferrari . . . my jaw fell open . . . C'mon . . . . was the response from him.

I am not shocked though I was earlier. After listening to him, as that was what I did most of the time when ever not in class of Mr. Tripaty's special lectures. Though boring, it used to be better than Rahul's lectures on his family . . . the heirloom . . . blood routes and the extravagant paraphernalia and royal air that hovered when ever Rahul was somewhere near. The lecture let me know there are families like his too; where rich remain rich. But that wasn't his intention though . . . he wanted me to know and understand his family.

Far, the soaring sound of emergency alarm ascended . . . *"My . . . . its 7 am . . . . I am gonna be late for Tripathy's bla bla . . . . class. Mom I'm off. No breakfast"*

Taking the keys I slipped off home before my mom followed with the lunch box. She believed I was still a kid and that pissed me for sure.

"Yes . . . Pick Gracy on the way . . . well she's my best friend and the worst when it comes to a critical situation . . . definitely a flip flop but good soul." I couldn't stop smiling and pressed the gas.

Surely late for the lecture but "Tripu" as Gracy refers wasn't in class. Taking the call, we reappeared at the hot spot-CANTEEN

It was surely a CAN TEEN. Look around you could see tons of teens gathered around. Finding a seat was a challenge. Today luck favored. Paaji's Samosa and Aloo Tikki with coke. The usual order and within minutes we were done with hogging ceremony.

"So wat's up with Rahul? Mmm mmm", Gracy popped her question followed by a weird expression.

"What???"

"Look at me naam se Gracy . . . Rahul pe crazy . . . and you . . . tell tell na . . . ."

C'mon give me a break this time. I'm truly, deeply, madly in love with that hunk . . . that's what you want right . . . take it. I wish I could eat every slice of him.

I stared at Gracy who got the message clear. In class a substitute was in place of Professor Tripathy. When not in classes the Bookers Park was my den. As the name, it was a park within the campus for those who preferred to read peacefully without being monitored as in the library. Note sharing, discussions and even occasional gup-shups took place here.

Trying to concentrate on the Fiction, I tried to scan the book into my memory. But nothing worked. Even switching seats and walking. Nothing worked. Finally, I decided to put away the book and took a magazine instead. Though a hobby at first, now magazines were inevitable part of my life style.

I wonder why all these women got themselves busy writing about their rotten past and pesky husbands. They flout their pair with pride and would definitely be treating him more pathetic than flies on rotten mango . . . poor souls. As long as the stories killed my time and boredom, they were just fine . . .

Minutes through the book Rahul appeared. Rahul . . . well one of the youngest millionaires . . . with great looks and poor brain make up. Would be better to take it as a manufacturing defect. We have been together since Day 1 of grad session and now being the 4th year . . . he is still the same. Very poor listener, autocratic to the core and a charmer to others for sure. He has been pestering me to meet his family. In 2 years the request had become a routine and a cause to break our conversation most of the days. Mr. Shishir Raizada owns a stake in almost all the industries nationwide. Mrs. Mrinali, his wife is a social freak and hardly has any time for home and the family. Sruthy their youngest is in the same college doing her grad.

Have met her few times but lately she too behaves odd kinda . . . nuts! Giggles for no reason . . .

Rahul . . . . a mystery. Unresolved . . . This is my life . . . Akruti style!

CHAPTER 2

*Life is a circus . . .
it must go on . . .*

Days of hardship seemed to taunt Akruti forever and she found it hard to believe she'd to move with this burden that weighed more as each day passed. Silent or rather lost for days she would keep staring at nothing . . . even the blank sky seemed to have no answers. Finally it was after lots of persuasion from her dad she was on to meet a therapist.10-That was the appointment with Dr. Dev. Skip the meeting . . . said her mind. On later thoughts and dad's request, she'd to tend the way. Not usual suggestion from a father but now his foresight paid off. He passed away a year later. He would have understood what would be of his little girl after he left.

Akruti recalled what she had anticipated of Dev and what she had found.

At 14 Rocks Ville Road, Anmod, the service road was less crowded or rather there were just 5 or less cars in the vast parking lot. She recalled.

She had ended up in wrong end of the city. Though all the busy roads in the heart of Goa are crowded with natives or tourists, this place seemed to be forgotten. In her faint memory, Anmod had great rock structures and resorts with nature's huge bounty. Finding the way to this no mans land took enough time. Admitting she was late, even in the well guided roads she struggled to locate the cottage and its looks gave odd vibes.

The door was heavily ornated and had a bronze bell instead of the normal calling bell we see.

'Bong' the bell sounded loud. But there was no response. She forced herself into the room at once and a pair of queer eyes and a stout figure with grayish moustache and semi bald head . . . (Sorry for the weird description) led her in. Thanking God for once, she apologized for the delay lying the roads were confusing.

"Please be seated in the reading . . . Sirji will meet you soon. He was waiting all this time for your arrival". It sounded more like a threat than a request as the sore voice groaned and he moved away muffling something. Bit relieved that he wasn't the person to be met; she seated herself in the living room.

Impatience built in and she got up to take a view of the room. The room was huge and had heavy curtains neatly bound. The sunshine partially swept the room through the white lace curtain beneath the heavy ones. The chairs were huge and the decor had a British touch . . . it should have been French as per the history of Goa but this was different. One side of the room was a mini library with all sorts of books ranging from Science to Suspense and Fiction. Even Nursery rhymes and Bed time stories were a part of the great collection. Little ugly fishes swam glee in a neat bowl of water. They seemed happy in the room. It was just her . . .

Time passed and it was half an hour wait. Without further thought, she picked up her bag and started to leave. The rush to exit the room ended in a thud. It hurt and suddenly the world just blacked out. When she woke, a pale face and a pair of curious eyes peered through neatly wiped goggles. The person, a man or rather a young fella must be in late twenties.

"Ouch my forehead . . ." she cried.

"Relax you've a deep cut there . . . that came from hitting yourself on the wall. Just relax. I have given you the pain killer. I am sorry for both the door and the wall had the same paint; a flaw from my poor workman". The gentleman winked

"How long have I been out of life?" . . .

"Just more than an hour or two" he chucked.

"Oh my . . . what the . . ." she tried to lift herself.

"Relax" . . . he helped her sit.

With great effort she carried herself and was off to the door

"Miss. Rai . . . I have called for Mr. Rai. He will be here to pick you"

"Kruti . . . Or Akruti . . . that's the way I prefer to be called" she retorted.

A moment of silence . . . then came "Kruti . . . Akruti . . . what ever I advice you to leave after Mr. Rai arrives".

"How dare he . . . and look at the air of retort" she mumbled.

"I was here to meet Dr. Dev. Well I see the old man has no time or value for his clients and have left silly assistants like you to handle a client"

A moment later the voice replied "ahem . . . well I'm Dev and I was in a conference call with a client abroad. Had been expecting you and when it was late couldn't keep myself away from helping yet another client."

Her face dropped. With a bundle of emotions brimming . . . shame, anxiety or regret or may be all that comes under the list of emotions, she remained calm.

"Now if would please be seated." He offered some coffee and she slurped it with least shame.

Slowly he started stepping into the main topic. Before he started, she broke the silence saying she'd nothing to discuss about.

He maintained silence till she relaxed and then confessed he was fully aware of her past from her father.

Her silence lasted longer.

She felt odd. She wanted to throw up or even pass out. For a relief she saw a familiar face. She joined her dad and on request left the place in no time.

At home there were anxious faces waiting. Mom and Aditi were very worried when they saw the bandage on her forehead. On being asked about the session at the doctors place, with nothing to share she replied, *"I would not be for further sessions"*

Sitting alone in the corner of the room and gazing the blank night sky, she tried to find answers. Answers were all she wanted. She recalled the day in 2006 when the call informed he is no longer a reality. She'd a vaccum within . . . More woes followed when she knew she was the guardian to his locker and account but why her? She wondered and the pressure ate her from within. She ate her grief and tried to act normal to all when she broke from within.

"I know I have to find the answers within me and no one can help me. The only way I can is to re-live my past . . ." she wept.

Love is like a breeze

She let the cool breeze fill her lungs. Pain was soothing for a change.

"Kruti" . . . a faint call . . . .

Someone has invaded my solitude . . . I tried to resist but a warm hand laid itself on my head . . . Hesitantly, I tried opening my eyes and dad was beside me. I know he has been worried about me since years but help was beyond my ability. All I could do is hide my inner self. Dad just smiled . . . he said nothing . . . but I could hear someone calling me . . . .

In a jerk my world toppled . . . dad wasn't there anymore. It was Aditi.

"Kruti are you ok? Are you still thinking about hotchy-pochy Mrinali? Chaddo didi. You know her well . . . . hey I wanted your help with my project. It's on Shakespeare . . ."

At times Aditi is a menace and has a quality to gaga non stop. Never empathetic. Now must admit it's a better state of mind. After all that happened today, Akruti pitied Mrs. Mrinali. She wasn't a part of them yet having traveled all the way from Mumbai to meet her, they deserve better treatment.

To heal her mind she'd been to the Infant Jesus Home and spent her time with the innocent faces. Whenever low she was there and Fr. Patrick in-charge of the orphanage led her to the church.

There he would allow her sit for hours, think, talk or even cry out her heart. Much has changed now. No tears. Back home, the Raizadas waited for her return. She's prepared this time and Aditi had given a hint about the visit. Shishirji was in his casual attire to suit his mood whereas Mrs. Mrinali had wrapped herself in a glittering silk with leather bag and matching assessories. Wonder how she manages to collect these artifacts she adorns herself with!

With a mild smile and few chit-chats, I managed to reach my room leaving mom and Aditi to take their turn to engage the guests. Sruthy had been waiting for me in my room.

"Hi . . . Bhaabhi I just thought . . . I mean we just thought we . . . were just passing this way . . . so"

The lady in peach salwar suit tried hard to explain why they had come.

"Save the reason Sruthy you are always welcome. So are uncle and aunty. How have you been? Busy with projects and seminars I guess?"

"Well bhaabhi". I had to break her asking her to leave the bhaabhi tag as it sounded weird.

"Call me Akruti . . . its fine"

Before she could proceed with the conversation Mrs. Mrinali barged into the room. I offered her a seat and she accepted. For few minutes there was no dialogue.

To break the ice, Sruthy started off complimenting her mom's sari and the new bag collection and Mrs. Mrinali joined in. She was so drenched in the trend that she was more a non-stop brand ambassador.

Few minutes into the topic, I felt odd and offered her tea. She took out a heavy bound photo album and said she wanted to share some family moments. I hesitated but Sruthy's face indicated persuasion and I gave in. Mrs. Mrinali sat beside me on the couch and started off with their wedding snaps and slowly the same moved to Rahul, Sruthy and their good times. Before she closed the book, she took few snaps and slowly put them back saying . . . "these are Rahul's favorites. Guess you wouldn't be interested anymore . . ."

I took the snaps from the pile. Rahul and me during our friend's wedding . . . he had forced me to take a best buddy snap . . . second one of all friends again Rahul, me, Sruthy, Gracy and a bunch of lunatics in Rahul's group. Third one was of us with the Raizadas at Sruthy's birthday and the last two of Rahul at his engagement accepting the Kanya dhan and a reception snap of the couple in their first dance. I couldn't help running my fingers over his face. So happy and chirpy. What had gone wrong?

Mrs. Mrinali and Sruthy had been staring at my face and with no idea of what was going on I shut the album. Mrs. Mrinali spoke up "that wasn't what I wanted you to see it's these . . . she flipped the photographs and the backside of each photo had a message. It read my love, with all friends and Krutz, rehearsal to engagement snap, big mistake and the embarrassment. For an instance I was dumb. I wanted to be alone and shared the mind with both the guests. Mrs. Mrinali left the room weeping but Sruthy stayed back.

I tried to escape Sruthy by gazing outside the window. Yet I was caught. She had learnt my mind.

"Din't you know what he felt for you? What happened in the final year? Do you know all the legal documents in the bank and companies hold your name with his? What is the answer to your solitude and silence?"

Then she broke into tears saying her mom hasn't been able to accept the truth about Rahul and still thinks he is somewhere suffering the splits-ville. She does remember the marriage Rahul had with Ankita, a doctor and Raizadas' family friend. The relation had lasted only for months and she was no where in the picture. Rahul had isolated himself and left for Europe to meet his friend and never returned. His friend's version said he was lost during sky diving and could never trace him.

Mrs. Mrinali has from then been gloomy, forgetful and at times weird and is under the impression that I'm the only one who can save her son and the one whom her son would communicate with. I had no answers to any questions yet after knowing about her, I had raised my tone on Mrs. Mrinali when she taunted my mom for silly reason.

With unanswered questions they left the house and I hoped the visit would be the last.

CHAPTER 3

Love is magical

At the Bookers park Rahul had already caught a place for me. He had invited me to attend a wedding. The groom was friend to both of us. But I had decided to skip the same. On pleasing, pleading and finally kneeling I had to give in. It was decided we add Gracy and Sruthy too. The next Friday we were off to Pune. The travel was tiring; yet Rahul had impeccable driving skill and did pretty good with the speed too. While Gracy and Sruthy spent time jabbing and hogging, I preferred to take a neat cat nap. I could notice the occasional stares Rahul would pass when any of his favorite tunes were played.

As ever ignoring was the best way to handle Rahul. He was a nut and a puzzle at the same time. On reaching Pune, we settled well in the rooms allotted to us and the day was spent partying and Sangeet ceremony full of music and dance.

The day dawned and there was a sudden hurry in the events. We were added to the family and taking up the role we tried our best to make the event a grand success. The wedding and phere went on fine . . . and post lunch the preparations to the receptions began . . .

We too had our share of break and enough rest. At evening we had some spare time and decided gup-shups with friends.

In between, I was asked to attend a call from home at the guest room phone and I excused myself from the chit-chat. Had 2 minutes walk to the room. The phone was on cradle and I expected a call at ay moment. All of sudden the lights went off; I was forced to wall. In the dim light that swept in from the garden outside I could see Rahul holding my arm tight.

"What the . . . . Leave my hand . . . oi . . . it's paining and . . . what" before I could complete he moved closer to me and even closer that I could feel his warm breath on my neck. I started panicking and was sweating in and out. Though I kept pushing him off, he bounced back . . . and he whispered "I fallen for you from the very first year of our college and tried ever since to make you feel the same for me. Sruthy and my parents are happy to have you as a part of the family but you. I want to know what you have in your mind. This was the only chance I had and promise me you accept me as your husband?"

I pushed him off and left the room qiuckly. Hoping no one had noticed and enraged by the way Rahul had behaved made me furious.

Back at the room, Sruthy and Gracy had waited with all smiles. I rushed to my room.

I was shivering and my heart ached . . . I wanted to call up dad and confess what had happened. I was scared, down with shame . . . What do I tell him and how? Questions never left me behind. Rahul has been a decent and has asked for my approval before he could meet my parents. Raizadas were wealthy and in no way we would make a match. I cried and the outpour lasted. Early morning, I took a bus to home without informing rest of the team and avoided all the communications with them, even if it meant to bunk classes. Raizadas visited dad with Rahul's wish. All my Dad asked me to do was to think and then decide . . .

Gracy visited me and gave funny excuses and ended up supporting Rahul. At night, 3 days after the incident, Dad sat beside me and sought my decision. After hours of discussion, I was declared as ruthless, unkind species and Rahul the saint.

Making up my mind, I left for college the next day and Gracy made sure I don't lose my temper. Rahul was not seen anywhere. I met Sruthy and heard Rahul had been worried and felt odd to meet me or call as he realized he had been nothing less than a roadside Romeo. He preferred staying at home and would ask if she met me.

"Bhai sees his life in you and he will be happy with you". Shruthy said and left.

Hiding my ego, I called Rahul and said "I'm fine". That was all I could say and yet these two words too came after my heart settled to a normal pace, else it would have burst off into pieces. We met the next day and the first words he uttered jolted me "Krutz . . . I didn't mean to. I'm sorry for what I . . ." Before I'd think of a reply, my lips were locked with his and he held me tight as though resistance never meant to exist. I realized that I loved him, yet I was ignorant. First kiss in my life. A man I had known for years. Happy parents. What more to expect? The magic lasted for few minutes and he was in tears. "I feared I would lose you forever. I swear I will keep you happy."

Everything in life seemed different and beautiful . . . but didn't last long.

Thinking about the days at campus and of course Rahul and our life together. Everything seemed so near and real . . . yet out of reach they went.

CHAPTER 4

Days of revival

A year passed. Once the wound healed, dad confessed Dr. Dev had visited a couple of times and checked on me. Thinking his presence would disturb me he had left quietly after discussion with dad. Now, I felt like an open book. Dad had told Dr. Dev every single page in my life and so did mom, Aditi and Gracy. Even Sruthy had given her share of information to him for better analysis. I felt cornered. "Am I insane? For God's sake I need help."

Dr. Dev is my only hope now and he is the only one who can help me. Before the sessions began, I had to vow to be at the sessions on time and foremost cooperate.

At Anmod, Dr. Dev was all set to start his session. I expected a grueling session made of rapid fire questions but in turn it was rather a casual visit. The first hour was spent in ice breaking where I had told him all about myself, likes and dislikes and the same came from the other end too. From the session it was evident that he's single and separate from his family. He was taken to be the mad man's doctor and his father's dislike towards the profession forced him to relocate to Anmod.

This went on for a week and occasionally, he would take me to beaches or the rock heights saying they too formed a part of the session.

The calmness reminded me of the chaos in college that I really missed. How fun it used to be . . . days where nothing in the world seemed to trouble or even matter to any of us . . .

After a couple of years in the same campus, everyone had changed. Some of them were friends yet others remained dormant and few belonged to no category. I still remember the first day in college. Gracy was almost lost and before entering the class we had bumped on each other. That was the first time we met.

Rahul . . . . he wasn't in my department. But first, he seemed to be an introvert kind . . . he had a mysterious charm. I admit. When ever I felt my heart pound faster with no reason . . . . Rahul was there.

It was kind of magic or rare chemistry where . . . the winds told me he was near and he was.

And when ever he was I lost myself to the winds and felt elevated to unknown world . . . that never existed.

It took more than a year for me to feel comfortable with Dev and he is surely Mr. Reliable. That's what Gracy feels too. Unlike what I thought, Gracy had been with me in the toughest time of my life.

Dev was no longer a guest. He used to visit me regularly and outings had become so common that we hardly remembered the progress of the session. We talked about nature, time, city life, traffic and even ant holes were topics of discussion. In between he would pop up questions about the college and life with Rahul and friends. By the end of the day, the session would end up as a research for him.

My own share of research did yield results about Dev and his relationship with a doctor in UK. He never went into details; yet was evident that there were pretty serious misunderstandings. But Dev being a simple person, I guess it could have been resolved.

Our session progressed . . . Its Friday. Every Friday serious schedule on the weekend outing is prepared and keeping enough time for family Rahul made his plans for the two days ahead. Quite calculative. I have started understanding him in depth. He was sure to spend time with family no matter what. This thought has a strong reason too. Rahul and Sruthy had been deprived from the care every child would expect and every emotion they experienced was measured and served in monetary terms which has left a bitter past for both.

I was early to college and Gracy had already been scribbling some pre lecture notes. I wonder what? The day's lecture was over by 2 and we spent couple of hours completing the lecture notes Rahul had to. Gracy's never famishing hunger took us to the canteen and we left for home. That wasn't the end of the day . . . . by 5, Rahul was on the street waiting for me and we left for the Bookers.

"What's your plan after college", he asked blankly . . .

"Find a good job", I replied.

"Why don't we get married?"

"No way . . . bachu you ought to be on your own before I nod a yes for the D day".

"But I'm sure I can take care of all your needs now too".

"Rahul . . . how can you expect me to live on your dad's money? Aren't you ashamed to even think of it?"

That did hurt his ego as he left the place without a word further. I knew I had been a bit hasty and should have handled the topic in a better way. I tried calling him on his number but he seemed to be in a rage and after failed attempts, I retired to my preps for the final papers.

Gracy stayed with me for combined studies and during this, the combination of snacks and rumors went rather more than studies. I did enquire about him but nobody had a clue. Sighing that he would have taken the advice in right spirit and would have thought to give his papers well, I relieved my self from his thoughts. I must admit not completely though.

Dad gave us enough support to clear the subjects. Aditi was barred from entering the room as she would never leave the scene if she does and mom's snack parcel was ever expected delight during the 3 week exam schedule. After every paper, I did wait for Rahul to turn up but he didn't. Each day I found very hard to concentrate and all the subjects I loved seemed to be boring to me. All thanks to Grace . . . she would keep me on the right track and her whacky doubts were pretty hard that I had to go through entire chapters to clear them.

The exams went on smooth and the Farewell Day came next. Bidding good byes and cheers to all, I waited at the Bookers for one last time. I tried calling him but the number was disconnected. I had no other way than asking Sruthy's help.

"Sruthy . . . could you ask Rahul to meet me ASAP???"

"You guys had a tiff heh . . . . I knew and he's been a brat since . . . Think he has done his exams well. Had seen him dusting his books before the exams . . . I will let him know when I meet him today." She giggled away.

I waited for the whole day and by six decided to leave as it was no use and safe sitting all alone there till night.

I know I had lost it and thought not to brood over the day's loss.

Rahul called me to meet him the next day. I denied.

On second try he said "it's either now or never!!" I felt he was into some trouble and met him at Costa . . .

It was after a month that we had finally met. And parted . . . I never knew for ever.

CHAPTER 5

The last meeting

Sipping hot coffee, I asked him "how did the exams go?"

There was a silence "Pretty good", he replied.

The dialogues continued . . .

"So this time little Raizada required no help . . . huh? That's neat".

"Don't call me by the family name . . . and yes, I have learnt to do my own stuff"

Rahul had changed and the change was evident from the way he revolted. A person who was airy about his bloodline boils over it?

"Sorry . . . I know I had been poking you around. I could have said this earlier."

"Akruti . . . forget it . . . I called you here to discuss about us and the future". Calling me by name surely created a great distance that had never happened.

"You preferred to get a job after college. Well I've my own plans for which I will be leaving the country."

"And may I know about your plans as you wanted a discussion on 'us' . . . ? I retorted

"Not now . . . I will keep in touch. Got to go. Have to pack my stuff too. Bye . . . I will miss you . . ." saying this he left me alone at coffee shop. I wonder he never asked how I'd been or anything related to me for that matter. He comes, talks and leaves.

Taking his dialogue easy, I left for home and that happened. Dad . . . Dad was in hospital. He had collapsed on this way to the office and was admitted. Mom could hardly talk. Putting Aditi at home, we rushed to the hospital. He had a minor chest pain. Though it didn't look minor to me or mom. He was out of danger and asked to rest for a couple of weeks.

I saw Dad getting older day by day and keeping his health in mind, I never discussed my worries with him the way I used to and each time he asked about Rahul, I said "he is finding a good job before he meets you" and he would smile.

I got my self placed as a freelance journalist with a local news paper and rest of the time did some guest lectures to keep myself away from thinking about Rahul. Days passed and months waxed away. I tried calling Rahul. There was no answer.

Tried Sruthy's number and she picked the call.

"Hi, this is Akruti. Is this Sruthy?" I tried to be polite.

"Where in the world have you been? I had tried to your number a couple of times . . . we need to talk . . ." she sounded disturbed and worried.

"OK Costa @11"

"Fine "she replied and the phone got disconnected.

I was anxious. The wait at Costa gave me an eerie feeling and my stomach rumbled.

The last meeting with Rahul had filled my thoughts.

Sruthy was there in no time and she settled down quickly with a pale face staring at me. She began saying,

"Hi . . . how much I wanted to meet you . . . what happened between you both on the day you asked me to pass your message? He left to UK very next day and has been giving much worry to the whole family".

I couldn't believe my ears . . . "Rahul really left? Well he had talked about his plans and . . . But . . . and what's with the worry? I hope he's fine . . ."

I tried to prepare myself for the second half . . . but the reply was fast and uncalled for.

"He got himself placed in a good job and . . . and . . . well"

"Well what?" my voice was loud but my heart pumped louder . . .

"He's married"

I felt frozen and in a minute my world went out of focus. I couldn't sit any longer and put my head on the table. I was no longer bothered of what others would think. Sruthy's palm felt heavy on mine. I tried to sit up.

"I know but I don't know . . . I mean I wanted to ask you about what had happened but this isn't the right time . . ."

She offered me a lift and I was pathetic enough to accept. On the way . . . I asked her why he had taken such a step and who was the person. I really wanted to know if there existed someone who could be a better suit for him.

She replied "perhaps you can answer the first half and Ankita, our family friend is a doctor in UK. Nothing was planned and I think bhai never wanted us to be at his wedding. It's just the photographs he sent saying he's fine." I got off and slowly paced to my home. Dad was at the living room but I swiftly locked the room door behind me. Dad must have sensed the problem. He was at the door in minutes. I had to face him and the very look at his eye broke my courage and I poured all my woes.

"Dad . . . I failed you and am a failure myself . . ."

"It's ok. We have to live against all odds . . . Life must go on dear . . ." he patted my head.

From the day I had nothing to share with any one or even confined myself to my room to avoid any questions or comments. Gracy tried to cheer my spirit but I couldn't help myself from thinking that I had become a worthless for all.

To break my thoughts I would work extra hours and retire to home late. That kept me busy and tired the same time . . .

Sruthy had called home and it was dad who took the message for me . . . he came to my room and fumbled.

Finally he broke the news that Rahul is no more. I can't remember what had happened after that.

When I woke up, I thought I was dead. I couldn't feel my body nor could move. Though blurred I could see only white and sharp lights were piercing my eyes. I shut my eyes and tried again. This time the picture was better. Dad and mom to my left . . . and a doctor. Or someone who looked like one. Aditi, Gracy, Sruthy, Shishirji and Mrs. Mrinali???What in the world is happening?

I could just blink. My lips were dry and mouth sore, throat ached and numbness prevailed. I tried to sleep. The doctor got my face wiped with ice cold water and I gasped for breath as if someone had clutched my throat. But I felt better in a moment.

I had passed out at home and was on fluids for a day. The workload and sleepless nights had run me down and Rahul . . . . that was a shock.

In a day, I was back at home. I saw both my parents were tired and they did look sick. Aditi had missed few classes. So, I had to push her to college. Gracy took a day's off till I felt comfortable and the Raizadas left after meeting dad. The night passed quickly. The next day Gracy started her usual chit-chat to which I was a poor listener. I hardly listened to her but when the name Rahul came in I was forced to hear . . .

"What about him and why in the hell do you want to discuss unwanted issues?"

"Krutz you must know all after Rahul left to UK, he was into some part timing stuff and it was during the stay there that he sought Ankita's help and what if they got married . . . . she was a ditcher . . . and his case was done in couple of months . . ." She sounded enraged.

"But why and how?"

"No body knows . . . I got to know from Sruths that he had mailed him about a break up and was on a trip with his friends in Europe when all this happened. He was broke . . . that's what she said . . ." Gracy frowned.

I had nothing to say and thought process in me had died. The only pass time I had was the window. See kids going to school, the vegetable cart being moved, sound of cycle bells and the sound of church bells."

Every night my Dad would sit with me saying bed time stories till I slept like I used to when I was little. Few days passed and I asked him to take rest and leave the stories as I felt better.

Mornings were boring and till Aditi and Gracy turned up, I would listen to the church bell and they would go gong every hour. Once Gracy was home, I asked her about the church nearby. Being a pious soul she said it was close by and had an Orphanage too.

Soon I was on the road to church. Gracy was as excited as a little child when she had me walk with her after so long . . . the last time was the farewell.

CHAPTER 6

@ Anmod with Dev

Dev broke the trance. Was I talking to him all this while? Time had passed and it was pretty dark. On our way we had a light dinner and were at home. Dev met dad and promised him I would be fine very soon as if I wasn't. With Dev, I had learnt to walk, talk and even smile. He did have a charm to change the mood and was good enough to play with minds.

After so long, I sat with mom and dad for the dinner and saw them smile each time I asked for more. Mom's food tasted exceptionally good and there emerged the joker. Aditi had been off with her studies and joined me for the dinner. It was a great feeling when all of us had food together. I told dad that the sessions were fine and did feel relieved of much pressure. The Orphanage and the kids there took my mornings as Gracy had helped me get a tutor job.

Dev was off on a convention and I spent my day time in helping mom. Never did I know cooking was so much fun. It was now that I knew; dad had changed his job and now works in a private firm. The bank job being far from home was tiring to him and the medicines had made him weak.

I have been out of family for pretty long time now. In my life, I was lost and the loss included my family too. But how did I not know anything that happened at home? On night fall . . . Aditi came with her notes for help.

Putting the notes aside I asked her to detail me what had happened to me and how I never knew any thing that happened at home. Finding the topic interested she put aside her books and started detailing on every single event after I'd collapsed. One whole year had passed and Aditi is due to complete her grad. I remember putting her admission forms for her and her first year in college . . . her complaints on ragging and freshers day but the final year . . . time flies!

I e-mailed to Dev every day and he would promptly reply with a remedy. Was he turning out to be more than a friend? Yes, I admit I need him and missed him but it was not love.

It was an attraction that forced me to move forward in life and I am not sure if I can move on without his support.

"Dev . . . I think Dad is unwell, and I wish you were here. I am not ready to take any thing life has set for me . . . not now for sure". I sent him a mail.

I was not sure if what I did was right by putting a good friend to choose between his career and a nut client like me. But he called.

"Dev Dev . . . . can you hear me. How's your project going?"

"Akruti . . . how's Dad? What's wrong with him?" He broke the intro. "I need you to listen to me. Just calm down and carefully understand what I'm going to tell you. You dad is sinking. He has a poor heart and it has worsened in the years. We never wanted to put hard facts in to you as you weren't prepared . . ."

I didn't respond . . . I couldn't

"Are you with me . . . Kruti . . . Kruti . . . are you there?"

"Dev . . ."

"Be with dad. I will be there in a day. Keep your mind open and be with family . . . take care"

I was trembling not able to know how I am to take the next step. What am I to do? I sat beside my dad. He looked pale and exhausted. He coughed occassionally. He had changed. I could no longer see my dad. Instead there was a pale elderly person with weak body and weaker mind. His eyes were wet, dark circles prominent and wrinkled forehead . . . Dad wanted to leave us?

Mom was brave. She had lived through the disease Dad had taken with him and she has overcome all the emotional turmoil. She stood beside me. Full of tears but silent. Aditi was calm as she has been well trained to by mom. I . . . what am I to do?

Hours passed and I still placed myself at his bed side. I called him slowly and he never responded. He gasped for breath occasionally and I was asked to give him water . . . slowly he relaxed and flexed his muscles. He looked calm and better than hours back. I wanted to tell mom he was fine . . . when I turned around she quickly left the room and cried aloud. Unaware of the fact my father had left the family for me . . . I kept staring at him. I believed he was breathing. If so, his chest would have puffed but he lay motionless yet calm. All I could do was kiss his forehead and say I miss him . . .

There was nothing but silence that scared me. Mom and Aditi tried to compose themselves and put me at ease. I wonder how they were able to do that. All my relatives were called for and for once I called Dev . . .

"Dev . . . He's gone . . . my Dad . . . he left" . . .

"God damn can you speak . . . silence is killing me . . . do something . . ." I yelled at him . . .

I could feel a hundred bees ringing in my ears and the whole world shook vigorously closed my eyes.

"Akruti . . . Akruti . . . please respond . . . hey are you listening . . ."

"Yes . . ." I think I replied . . . I'm not yet sure of it and he continued . . .

"Akruti . . . be strong. I want you to face the reality . . . Do you get me . . . you can not lose your self. You have to come back and back in full throttle. Dad wants to see you fine and happy in life where ever he is. Don't let your mind rule you . . . I will be there soon. Please take care . . ."

People came and went. The house seemed to be more like a museum to me. I saw faces everywhere and they had no emotions on them . . . Amongst them . . . I saw him . . . Dev.

I couldn't stop my self from crying my heart out. It was paining within . . . He sat beside me and held me tight saying . . . "I am here everything's gonna be fine . . . relax". Dev took over the situation and I was put on sedatives to relax and till the last rites were done. I was neither dead nor alive. I could hear mom and Aditi cry . . . sounds of conch, strong fumes of incense . . . I couldn't move.

Things were back to usual in weeks but the vaccum dad has created couldn't be filled. Mom had got back to her kitchen and she spent more time in meditation and Aditi tried to get her self back into the semester exam preps. Dev was busy with his clients and I had asked him to pause the sessions till I was ready and he agreed.

For a change, Gracy and I left to meet Father Patrick. His words gave peace of mind. On our way, I decided to spend some time in the park.

The foot fall was low. The climate was slightly windy but could manage without sweaters. Seeing green all around me soothed my mind.

"Oh my . . . what was that?" . . . I felt insecure and. It was soothing but . . . . the winds just gave me Rahul for a moment . . . I got up and ran around the park . . . couldn't see any one . . . perhaps my mind is still hovering in the past . . . Dev is the remedy.

Saturday 10 a.m.

I was at Devs' and shared with him what had happened at the park. He stared at me for few minutes . . . and then said "Akruti . . . how in the world can a woman be so very crazy about a man who had left her for someone else . . . you are so much filled by him and have lost yourself in him . . . How am I to find you without finding him?"

I sighed and said "I ponder a lot over my dead past".

"Kruti . . . if I can call you so . . . I think we need to find a solution to your trouble and it's high time we get to the next level. We will have to find start things from where you had left for that's the start of a new chapter in your life."

"Dev . . . I will have to think and find my way out. The doubts Sruthy has been holding, the belief Mrs. Mrinali held that I knew about her son . . . Ankita and the whole collapse . . . need to sort the pile"

CHAPTER 7

Self realization that I was madly in love

"Dev . . . What do you think love is?" For this one time I wanted to know what he felt and how he describes the emotion or the feeling that gifts abundance of joy drives you to paradise and mesmerizes you and the same time could kill you in an instance with a broken heart . . . .

"Now that's a tough one . . . . I think it's just a breeze which can't be stored and is better if left free . . . what's your version of it? I know everything about your past. How was it when you guys first met? Was it sparking or did you get to know more about each other to realize the cupid effect?" I smiled. I thought he was joking . . . more than 1000ft above the floor on a cliff top when our legs dangling towards deep forest.

"Hey . . . I'm not joking . . . I really would like to know . . . but if it wouldn't hurt you . . ."

I couldn't deny Dev even if it meant treading through the patches that still hurt. I asked him if he was sure and he just nodded.

The winds gave a chill and the yellow sky had slowly turned purple giving way to the night sky. I took a deep breath and my lungs were full . . .

"I was a normal person until he came and made me feel special . . . I believed love was a lie until I had met him. I knew happiness but he gifted me joy without horizon . . . I smiled and he found out ways to make me smile always . . . each day. I could feel him in the gentle breeze, in the white clouds and even in the fresh drops that drizzled.

I've always wondered why this happened only with Rahul . . . there were many guys in college who were my good friends . . . yet none of them made me feel restless, confused and lost."

In the first year there was just an attraction but each day the magic seemed to take me over and still I could attribute it to be pure friendship or more . . . but not love. I had full freedom with him . . . call him talk to him at any hour and rely on him. He had a style and tricks to sort any issue impeccably . . . mine or of his friends.

The year break used to be terrible without any friends. Gracy was the only source of entertainment . . . the chatter box would be active 24x7.She has weird topics and gossips to discuss. More an entertainment glossary . . . choose and you get it. The 2nd year started with much fun . . . expecting lots of new faces into the campus. This time the seniors were put together in Wellington Block to avoid any cases of ragging or misconduct from the senior bunch. This was the first step towards a unity amongst all groups under grad course.

It was new line of a fine poem too . . .

We met . . . all good buddies together . . . Amongst all the faces . . . moving in and around the block . . . my eyes searched for him. Hanging out with his folks, I'd look at him; his smile and charm . . . true prince . . . no wonder so many of lady bugs buzzed around him . . .

Each time he would pass a glance, I would escape them pretending to be busy with my own jing bang . . . as weeks passed . . . the glace turned to smile and this time . . . I tried my best to return one too.

The monsoon . . . they always remain fresh in my heart . . . . On break of monsoon . . . I would enjoy juggling the rain drops from the parapet . . . and this time I wasn't alone . . . I saw a pair of dreamy eyes staring at me . . .

He waved and I rushed to the dormitory. I never knew why . . .

The next we met was at the canteen . . . Gracy was a better friend of his and they did spend some quality time together. It was Gracy who sowed the seeds. She introduced me to Rahul for the very first time . . . we talked . . . he was courteous . . . gentle and considerate.

We talked more about anything and even nothing.

He made sure he didn't miss any event I had invited him and I made myself present in all his soccer matches . . . not for the game I'm sure. Every time he glanced, my I could hear my heart . . . louder than anything. We spent time together making reasons . . . common subjects, note sharing, and birthday party. Even if India won or lost in the cricket match . . . it was either winners treat or cheer up group.

Gracy usually accompanied either of us and seeing the trend move to daily meetings she excused us and we were best friends

We never celebrated Valentines fearing the concept would break our friendship and more.

I knew I loved him but I wasn't sure about it . . . I was nuts for him but only he knew his mind . . . but his silence gifted me dreams that filled up my days and nights. So many times I have wondered . . . how day dreams would be and I learnt them through him . . . Listened to all his stories whether true or silly . . . his smile was where my life would be and his hand was the trust . . . and his eyes my faith . . .

I started liking him so much that I wanted to know him more. It was Gracy and Sruthy who helped me. And on their question why I did so much investigation about him my answer was "to be great friends we ought to know them in and out".

Every time Gracy and Sruthy joined me at the Bookers, he would turn up with an excuse and pick Sruthy or Gracy. I never knew why . . . but Gracy knew . . . that's when she asked me at the canteen about what was going on . . . I feared the magic is out of the box. I loved it to be secure and safe even from my close aides."

Sruthy . . . she is good. I mean very good . . . . holds a beautiful heart.

"I know . . ." Dev jumped excited . . .

"Dev . . . ." I gave a stare and he asked me to continue . . .

"Sruthy she was so innocent and was bad in keeping secrets. She changed with every meeting we had and I was forced to think what made her giggle and her reply to Gracy was that her bhai had been asking about me lately and has given the same useless reason . . . "to be great friend . . .""

"Gracy . . . . I've heard of good friends, close friends and even best friends . . . now what's a great friend???" Sruthy commented.

I knew it was a genuine poke on the wrong way . . . . and Gracy's contribution added to my worry "Well . . . . lately there's kinda virus stuff that turns friends into sub and main categories the way milk is turned to curd or even Paneer . . . sluuurp . . . . I love paneeerr . . . yumm . . ." Gracy smacked her lips.

The lady hopped around me and stopped at once . . . "Krutz . . . what's your take on the virus??? Is it good or fatal?"

I was dumb. I felt as if I'd swallowed a frog.

I smiled and thought silence would be the best response. That gave both the dame a chance to pull my leg when ever possible and to me that was a regular session. All of sudden Sruthy seemed to have caught the bhaabhi hiccup and she used to do the same in public each time she saw me. I had to taunt her for that few times but the nut wouldn't' break. I had to ignore or follow her conversations when we met irrespective of what she called. But I kinda enjoyed the wit too.

Those never stopped us from meeting . . . if my intentions are pure then why fear? I thought. All was good except the lifestyle the Raizadas which had disturbed me from getting closer. I feared the future. I wondered if he would also turn into an inconsiderate rich brat. At times, I did wonder why I'd thought so much for him. The day and the few moments we spent at the wedding, changed my life for ever. I could no longer hold myself and felt untrue each time I tried to convince myself that nothing called love existed. I lost it . . . I was in it already and trapped for a life time not knowing how to get myself out of it . . . till this very moment."

I felt warm. My face was wet with tears . . . and Dev gave me a hug saying now his session worked. He wanted me to open up and let my heart lighten or even cry.

Wiping my tears, Dev said he too had an affair at college and that broke just because her fiancé wouldn't let them get married . . . we broke into laughter at once . . . I never believed he had such a silly story. This time he swore "I am single and gladly have no broken heart. Thank God, He saved me from complicated women like you. Imagine my girl friend's fiancé chasing me with a butcher's knife . . . all ready to slice me into kheema . . ."

Though emotionally tough day . . . I felt much better. I learnt yet another truth Dev likes Sruthy and he's genuine. I'd definitely give him an ISI trademark in character if there were any. He's a true gem. I will have to know Sruthy's mind before I jump into any conclusions.

CHAPTER 8

Ricky vs. Life

Wednesday 9.00 am

A black sedan pulls over to the parking lot. A sturdy figure steps out and rushes passed the tulips on the pavement to the Clarks Tower at Burlington. Taking the stairs to the eleventh floor didn't tire him a bit. Pushing the tinted glass door with all might, he barely notices the cubicles and the people out there, and finds his way into the well designed cabin and Jane quickly follows his pace with the day's schedule. The masculine figure enters his private office, a designer living area to suit his taste and to a corner stood a work table comprising of the most sophisticated correspondence kit and a laptop for his personal use.

Once Jane was done with her briefing about the day's time slot, he spoke . . . "That's it right? . . . no alterations".

Well groomed hair and fair complexion were subordinated by his stern look that always has been a fear factor to his team. He was in his usual style . . . well tailored suit and neatly done face which shone no emotions. The deep scar on his chin and forehead was a mystery to all his peers.

He wasn't kind but never ruthless either. If he were, the Sunday Schedule wouldn't have a visit to the Child Home that never got cancelled. The visit was a code red agenda maintained by Jane. Though she had never been to the Home herself . . . she stood second in line of authority to deliver the message and package in case he couldn't make it to the appointment due to his meetings abroad.

That was the level of privacy Ricky preferred.

Even after being a leading media bug he was never in limelight and preferred to stay the way himself.

"Janet fix my meeting with Mathias and the coffee", he said firmly.

Ricky was the only person in the world who called her by her true name and she was grateful to him for reminding her name while others stuck to Jane.

Jane scurried from the room and Ricky was back at his desk to attend the mails and the voice mails. First thing in the laptop he clicked open the jpeg file (perhaps the only one) and let his eyes scan every pixel of it as if he had had it saved to his memory.

It was a year back Jane had picked up the courage to ask about the picture, mishap when she was to install the mail protector software. And the response . . . a day loss of pay for invading his privacy.

Before Jane entered, he was done with his correspondence and had his eyes fixed at the wish fountain across the Tower. He was seen lost in his world and this would happen daily. Jane had learnt Ricky pretty well and knew that this was the time she could clear the approval and the employee grievance files. Jane, a cheerful soul had been with Ricky for pretty good time and had handled almost all issues in the firm with utmost precision.

Ricky could confide in her any issues yet the heart of the man she admired remained a puzzle. She did earn grudge for not revealing any secret of the boss and protected Ricky from any rumors that aired and had always been a close aide to him.

CHAPTER 9

Dev loses himself

I sank deeper into the memory stream and tried to find out what went wrong between us. For once I decided to visit the Raizadas and left to Mumbai. Dev accompanied me to avoid any kind of emotional torment. He feared a torment would collapse all the efforts he had taken to bring me back to normalcy. We were at the palatial house of Raizadas. I was hesitant going into a house where I had nothing to expect. Yet had to move on to trace the truth. Mrs. Mrinali as usual was out socializing and Shishirji at work. Sruthy was absolutely gaped. This visit was least expected.

"Bhabhi . . . I mean Kruti ji."

"Just thought to visit you all and see your mom. I had been a bit rude the other day at my home . . . Sorry for the mishap."

She offered us tea and snacks that did relieve to a great level the exhaustion from the journey. I blankly asked her for the photos Mrinali auntie had brought the other day and that I wanted answers to all the doubts in her mind at the earliest. Dev went through the photos and the comments while discussing about her education and future plans.

I wonder if he had joined me to clear my doubts or flirt with Sruthy.

"Dev . . . If you are done I would like to have a word with Sruthy in private"

Dev silently left us to talk and now it was my turn to speak.

"I am going to answer all your questions very soon and you can trust me this time . . ." I assured her.

"Tell me one more thing. As you know about Rahul and me is there anything you would like to share with me?"

Sruthy blushed for a moment and then replied . . . "Bhaaabhi you na . . . Nothing . . ."

"What do you think about Dev? He is my buddy boy and a true gem. I think he . . . na I'm sure he likes you but I will surely ask him not to flirt with"

"Oh no . . . bhabhi bhabhi . . . it's not like that. Don't scold him please. I mean I like his character and he has helped you a lot I see"

"I just want to know if you guys are really serious . . . and I would be happy if it be answered in a yes or no".

"Yes bhaabhi . . . I like him but I'm not sure what parents would think . . ." she replied worried.

"That's my role . . . . soon we'll meet with good news. Take care dear". Giving her warm hug and saving more conversation for the next visit we left Mumbai.

With each mile we traveled . . . the greenery vanished . . . giving way to more dusty roads and view kept altering before any of it could get registered. Rahul left lots of stones unturned and the path he had chosen left none happy. Instead lives that burned brought out fumes of despair, woes shattering expectations and breaking hearts. I am no exception. Sruthy had been Rahul's strength and weakness as well. Yet he left her to an unknown future. And the parents who would have been hoping their son would take up their responsibility have also been fooled.

What would have made him let the ties off that he had tried hard to get bound? He never sounded unsure about us too. It was hard for me to decide how I am going to sort the mess and the time that flew without any bounds . . . too much of unsurety existed in and around me.

I was sure of the fact that I have to fix everything to answer my soul that irked suspicion. Dev for a change kept himself calm and concentrated on the road for a change. He would have realized my effort to clear the cluttered mind.

The trip back never seemed exciting as my thoughts were lured. And lured towards everything I wanted to forget. The truth being every time I tried to forget, I kept remembering it.

Aditi had kept a sulky face and Mom tensed. I had to keep aside my bundle of thoughts. Post dinner, Aditi and I joined mom in her too. I could read she had something to say and that she clearly hesitated. On nagging she put the topic of my future. And evidently marriage . . . the long term commitment. I maintained silence.

"Kruti . . . I'm getting old and would wish to see both of you well off and I can rest. Dad would have thought the same. I believe I'd given you enough time and I am convinced about Dev. For Aditi your uncle has found a good alliance. He is a software mechanic . . . or engineer . . ."

My eyes bulged out and glad that I wasn't alone. Aditi too had the same face with minor alterations though.

"Mom Dev???? For God's sake . . . he shouldn't hear this . . . . he would run away for his life".

"Ma . . . What does Mamaji have to do with my life I want to be working and have my goals set ma . . . . a world class journalist . . . media head . . . . and have a long list ma . . . ." Aditi moaned.

"Now . . . enough I don't want to listen to any reason and why would Dev run? What's wrong? And why wouldn't he like? You have been with him for quite long and he knows you more than any one." She sounded desperate.

"Aditi . . . I have to talk to mom, please wait for me at my room", she left or rather hopped off in fury.

It was high time I clear mom's worry.

"Maaa . . . I know that I've been a trouble child with my decisions. But Dev and I . . . I mean we are not together . . ."

"What not together? Din't you go all alone with him to Mumbai?" She retorted.

"Maa I mean we were together not in the sense you take it to be. He is good and the best husband anyone could have, but not mine. We are friend and he is my therapist maa. I wouldn't want him to take me as a burden all his life though he wouldn't mention".

Mom wasn't completely done . . . "but he is good . . . I thought you would be happy with him where ever you are".

"Maa", I held her hand tight "where am I going to leave you for the world and why have you agreed to

Mamaji about Aditi? She's just a kid and has to go a long way . . ."

Mom smiled and her voice cracked . . . "She is 23 and no longer a child. I wish I could see you both happily married and had wished to be with bhai for he's all alone at the village. If I am lucky we would get a chance to re-live our past and spend the rest of our life together. Aditi . . . she is no longer a child . . . I say this again 'cos she has been seen with some boy with spiky hair by some of our neighbors and it's the same you said about Dev that she too has found for a reason. What am I to do now? You both decide if you want to keep me happy the rest of my life and die peacefully or leave me to suffer".

She muffled and broke into tears. From under her pillow she had pulled a folded envelope. It was the job offer to UK. I had applied long back when the jobs were gone and I'd talked to dad about taking up a project abroad. This had a hand of Fr. Patrick too. He had recommended me as a sincere social worker and an academecian. I really don't know what the term academician meant and what my role was.

The project was for a year and could be extended upon request and would include education to the under previlidged. The first few months would be training sessions and surely traveling.

CHAPTER 10

A well awaited change . . .

Aditi anxiously waited for me in my room. Pulling the wraps and making sure the mood was right I told her about the assignment I'd got. She wasn't surprised and in turn held that a reason for mom to get her married off early.

I had to play the big sister now. I asked her about the spiked head . . . and she blinked . . . "Di . . . you're a genius. How did you know about Virat? Did you meet him? What did he say? Did you like him . . . I know you would have liked him . . . like I did" her bullets aimed at me were shot at once. Before she could bury me I'd to interrupt.

"I don't know Virat. Neither did I meet him. Mom knows about the affair and for a change, I'm not sure if I'll like him if he's your choice"

Aditi sobbed.

"But if you take me to meet him . . . I can reconsider . . . . if you will" I assured her my help and she smiled as if she had won the whole world. I couldn't help smiling. I know what she'd be feeling . . . the joy that had surrounded me years back.

The very next morning skipping breakfast, we were off to meet Virat. He was indeed spiky. But looked fine.

After the intro we sat for a coffee. Aditi was all smiles and blushy. I felt awkward sitting between two people who had known each other well enough to choose to share their future.

Virat seemed like a gentleman and he talked all about himself. Starting from his family to the fact that he was a free-lance photographer and did projects with Big names in media apart from being full time Software Administrator with the leading IT firm.

Leaving nothing to be asked, I excused myself asking him to talk to mom in a week.

At home, I told mom about Virat and informed that they would be here to meet her in a week. It was a bit tough to convince her, but the fact that Virat was an IT person had solved at least one of her demand. The rest would fall in place and it did. They were home the next day and Aditi was betrothed awaiting my marriage to set the date for her own. All of it happened pretty soon.

I had to convince them that I'd a project abroad and would be happy if they could do the nuptial early. I could leave then and mom will be with her brother too. Virat opposed saying would wish to wait for six months to make sure he was well organized with his assignments and work patterns before he would take Aditi. And the date was decided. My little Aditi will be married in few months.

Mom seemed less happy. She was still brooding over my future. "Mom . . . dad had applied for this job and I'd want to join them for few months at least. You needn't worry at all. It's Mamaji's responsibility to find someone for me by the time I'm back and if you approve you may give them your word. Your decisions would be my destiny maaa" and hugged her.

She smiled "I won't decide. Dad has never disagreed to your wishes ever. And I won't either. Promise me you will be back soon and will not decide to stay there for ever as you know I can not go against your wish and I won't be happy either. May I ask why not Dev?"

"He is Sruthy's maa . . . I will talk to the Raizadas before I leave", I winked at her.

I couldn't wait to meet Dev. On my way to meet him, he called . . . "Kruti . . . I need to see you at once. I will leave for your home right away . . ."

"Woo . . . woo . . . Dev. I'm already on the way. Meet at your place in 5, 4, 3 minutes". The door was open and Dev was anxiously waiting for me.

"Kruti I want you to see something and come in . . ."

"Dev Dev . . . later . . . Aditi is engaged. It happened all of sudden and she will be with Virat, her love in next 6 months. You are the next and I'm gonna take you to meet the Raizadas tomorrow . . . I have no much time left . . ." had just time to take a sip of coffee . . . that was ready.

Dev had a funny look on his face . . . "What's happening? Aditi is engaged . . . all of sudden without any notice? And what about not having time?" . . . I extended the letter towards him and his eyes were wide open . . . so was his mouth . . .

He sank to his couch with his hand on this forehead. I wondered how my trip could worry him . . . Don't tell me he'd miss me . . .

"Dev . . . . what's the matter? What's disturbing you?" He placed an enlarged photograph on the desk before me.

It was Rahul's weddings snap . . . doing the rituals. I wondered what was with Dev and why he had enlarged this particular photograph. I tried to avoid questions on it and simply asked why he had called me.

Dev had no emotions on his face "So . . . Ms. Rai will be to UK soon and she never bothers to inform me . . . Oh . . . I'm just a therapist . . . perhaps she is fine now and there isn't any need for further suggestions too", he sounded indifferent.

"Dev . . . it's not like that mom wanted me" . . . "If mom wants you may . . . why in the world would that be my problem?", he interrupted.

I knew it wasn't the right time to talk and left for home.

The next morning seemed to be hard to spend. I had nothing in particular to do. Took Aditi for shopping and had been to meet Gracy. Lady had been busy with her own commitments and soon would be a mom. So I preferred her being with her family rather than taking visits to my home now and then. We talked and talked a lot after a long time. The assignment as for all and me was a surprise to her but she was happy I was able to think future and that too in a positive note.

Aditi took full privilege of being younger to me by churning out my bank balance for her shopping frenzy, but she was happy and only that matters to me. Mom had always been cautious about the spending pattern especially after dad left us and the chances of shopping were turning out to be dreams to Aditi.

Dev was home and mom had been a great host. I could see from the empty snack plates too. He smiled and I gave a stare. Mom was disturbed and looked at Dev nodding her head. What is she nodding a no for? Dev gave her a mild smile and turned toward me.

"Kruti, I'm sorry for I was not done with my sessions and your decisions came to me as a shock rather than surprise. Mom told me about her wish and how Aditi's engagement happened. Yes, I agree . . . it happened all of sudden and it is a great opportunity you have got . . . could have been good to me by hinting me about the same . . . first."

I turned away from him and he followed me to the door . . . "Kruti let me tell you I'm happy for you and we need to talk."

"About what? And before anything, I would like to know when we will meet the Raizadas?" I put forward my demand.

He replied "Raizadas tomorrow, my mom will be in Mumbai, we pick her from airport and then meet the Folkers . . . I mean Raizadas. But before that . . ."

He pulled me to the tea table and put Rahul's wedding photo on it and asked me to have a look at it carefully.

"What do you see?" He asked anxiously.

"C'mon Dev why do you hurt me so much? Does torture be a part in your therapy?" I cried. I wanted to leave and remain alone.

He dragged me back and the same question came . . . . "Kruti see that snap and tell me what you see . . . ."

"It is a wedding snap and the groom who happens to be Rahul is doing the rituals at his wedding and the bride is all smiles . . . Would that answer you Dev??? Now . . . leave me alone . . ." I got up to leave.

Dev was calm now. He sat beside me and asked me to look at the same photograph. I wonder what he had in his mind.

"Kruti . . . see carefully the ritual . . . its Kanya dhan . . . and see his hand . . . I mean Rahul's hand . . . his hand is over the bride's hand and he isn't wearing a decorative pagdi . . ."

I felt he was absurd . . . "now what difference does that make . . . he wouldn't have got one".

"Offff . . . Kruti you are impossible . . . Rahul is doing the Kanya dhaan he isn't the groom . . . he is acting brother to the bride . . ."

In a moment . . . . I wondered why this never struck me and the realization turned the world hay wire . . .

"You mean that Rahul . . . . but how can we be sure?" I asked. "I am" Dev said affirmative.

"We have to start our quest from this photograph. It is indeed a coincidence that you wanted to take me to Raizadas . . . I would have gone myself today, if you hadn't met me yesterday. We have to talk to the Raizadas about this. We might get our next track from there.

Be ready, I will pick you at 9 sharp tomorrow. Have talked to your mom about this. Don't worry everything's gonna be just fine." He assured.

The hours to morning were blank. I had lost my ability to think. Dev was punctual and soon we were on the road to Mumbai.

"Will this work Dev . . . and he is no more so what change does this trail make . . . ?"

Dev kept a calm face and replied . . . "Knowing a person you have loved for your life has not betrayed you till his life . . . . don't you think that makes a change Kruti?"

I made myself easy on the seat and closed my eyes . . .

CHAPTER 11

Jane @ service

Far in the serene suburb of Burlington, A neatly painted cottage stood with magnificent glow. Though suburb it never had scarcity in the population. The neighbors never disturbed him yet suspicions invaded about the gentleman who had been living all alone. He had no visitors except a lady who turned up once in a week or never at all. He would smile at them occasionally but mostly kept a plain face and remained a bad socialite.

The garden had been well maintained and the large stones neatly led to the dark teak door. Behind the door, a world barely known to the outer world existed. The rooms were richly colored and had an imperial touch. The furniture was a combination of French and British origin. The cottage had all other than right hands to tend them. The structure had been renovated and Brit style had been converted to rich gothic structure. The answering machine beeped loud . . . .

"Boss . . . the meeting with Mr. Mathias has been fixed and he is expected to meet you at office in an hour". In a sudden jerk Ricky rose from the bed and rushed to the phone. In a minute the conversation was over and Ricky rushed to the coffee maker. In minutes he was done and outside Jane had been ready to rock the road with her Lamborghini. She had dreamt of one and seeing the lady's loyalty and her contribution Ricky gifted her the vehicle. She owed him her dreams and her whole life. When her life had seen the darkest times he had been standing by her to lift her emotionally and financially.

On the way, he browsed the news paper she had kept for him and a brief update of the day's schedule was done. Sipping the Costa she had picked on the way to appease her rumbling tummy, she glanced at the mirror to see what her boss was up to as she drove.

As usual he maintained his placidity.

"Boss may I dare to ask you about your family?" She had to pick up all her guts to spill out the words she had just said.

"Janet", he responded blankly.

"Do you have to be reminded about the penalty? If it is a must I am on for it".

"Boss . . . just concerned . . . I've known you for years now. But not of your family. Don't you feel lonely?"

"Thanks for the concern. I'm fine. It'd be great if you could get us to the meeting early", he answered her fairly well that no further doubts or questions came from the driver.

Jane's doubt had twitched his mind yet he focused on the meeting ahead of the short trip. He had trained himself to keep his mind disunited from his work. As a solace what he held was the picture in his laptop. In midst of any distress the image was the only medicament that could bring him back to normalcy.

The meeting with Mathias had concluded in a positive note. Asking her to leave for the office; Ricky took a cab to his hangout: the cafe facing the fountain. Though few steps from his office, he'd never be there in work hours and would spend his wee hours of morning sitting near the fountain letting himself be rejuvenated by the sound of water and the droplets that mildly ran through his face. The mist and the sound of gushing water always gave him his lost love. Realisation is a slow process but when it strikes him, his hands first ran over the scars and would get back to his cabin before anybody noticed him.

Jane had seen him by the fountain during her early visits to open the day's work but could never relate it to his persona. At times, she even thought him to be a psychologically disturbed or an over stressed. All she would do was try to make his day a relaxed one by handling the issues that could be resolved with all her might and would let the tougher ones to be handled by him.

Ricky was back at his office. He tried a number on his mobile and remained silent. The call was on mute for few seconds. He closed his eyes and put the phone back on cradle. His eyes were moist and his throat ached as if it were being strangled.

Just as Jane entered the cabin with the coffee, she was perplexed by the very sight . . .

Ricky was on the desk. His body inclined on the high chair and eyes closed. He had perspired heavily yet the thin stream of water originated from his eyes shown indication of tears. The neck tie was undone and he was pale.

"Oh my . . . is he asleep? Or . . . is he ill?" She murmured and rushed towards Ricky with a glass of water. "Sir, are you OK? Do you need a medic? Shall I get something for you?"

Ricky slowly opened his eyes and wiped his face with a cool towel he had kept ready. He used them when he was totally drained with the amount of work or when he felt he was falling for the stress. Calling it a day . . . he left for his cottage, not waiting to answer Jane. All he said was he's fine and would work from home.

At home . . . Ricky unlocked the door which even his servant was prohibited from entering. He laid at ease on the rocker. With a click the curtains dropped and music was on. His eyes were fixed on the huge portrait on the wall. She has suffered enough and deserves a happy life. Years have passed. She would have sought for a great life. He was a dead man to the world and his past had nothing left for him to think of. I have no right on her and hence why give her the misery to live with a man bearing ugly scars. He ran his hand over his face as his mind hovered over his past.

He closed his eyes tight and tried to sleep. Even when eyes closed he could see only one face . . . a face so fair and smooth . . . The first time he saw her . . . 10 years back . . . the trip with friends to Goa had changed his life for ever . . . the view of the beach from the resort balcony was pleasure to the eyes added with each sip of chilled beer. It was during one such evening . . . he saw her and only her . . . a normal girl. Pale white complexion. Cute little eyes, sharp nose and a smile that he would even die for. Not able to hold himself, he screamed from the balcony . . . "hey . . . hey you . . . there . . . what's your name" . . . there was no response.

The act had become a joke for the rest of the journey.

The next day he waited for her . . . this time without the beer. He had even believed the beer had done some mischief on him, making him think of a girl who never existed. But she came. He gasped for breath. She was real. He gazed at her without blinking . . . . her baby pink salwar suit that held tightly to her petite structure. She looked like an angel . . . her hair swayed in the breeze and her thin long fingers tried hard to keep them aside.

She was beautiful and by every passing minute her beauty drew him to her and for once he wanted to see her close enough. He ran to the beach and this time towards her . . . she gently passed him and her hair gently ran through his face. He believed he was in heaven for that one nano second.

What more can a teenager do? He followed her silently where ever she went and found her home.

Since then his every vacation included a week's stay at Goa. Soon, that had become a routine affair. With every visit her glow grew and the charm increased. He was under spell he believed . . . a spell that gave him immense joy that no other thing in the whole wide world could give and a crave to know her more and see her more . . . . With the spell, he grew . . . so did she and it was for her he chose a college nearby to have more time with her.

The first day in college, his eyes had searched for her and only her and once it met, he was taken . . . Every time he saw her she would shy away and every smile was carefully captured. So were her innocence and even her naughty glance.

Studies were second when it came to how he could get to know her and talk to her.

From the very moment he met her, he had stitched her to his heart and was sure if he had a family she was there for sure. At college, seeing her more he had been familiar to her and he believed her to be no different from him. He had tried to keep his calm to add his courage to talk to her. He thought of ways to get to her and it was for sure through her friends. He was thought to be a lunatic by his good ol buddies for his crazy love for the dame. He would smile and answer . . . "If there is heaven, it is where she is . . . if there is God . . . she is the one and if there is air . . . it's her scent . . . she's my love, my life and my death too".

"And do you know if she is love with someone else?"

Imran popped the question he had feared for years. He had no answer and without an answer she was not his. It was high time he confessed his state of mind to her.

CHAPTER 12

Meet the Folkers day for Dev

Kruti had reached Mumbai. Taking a halt for snacks, she called her mom to inform that they had reached safe. An incoming call from Gracy lit her face.

"Gracy I'd wanted to talk to you and must say I miss you especially when it comes to trips like these. I have to tell you more" and the call continued till they had reached the airport.

Dev's mom was a great mother. She had been with him always and it was Dev's decision to ask her stay with dad to make sure his dad wouldn't have to bear the brunt of not approving the medical career. She was chubby and has a great smile; no wonder Dev has one too. We picked her from the airport and made sure she was fine to travel further. Got a room booked at a hotel in the city and later in the evening, we left for the Raizadas. My heart pound heavily; not because I knew a secret about Rahul but I was not sure if the Raizadas would approve the proposal for Sruthy and I am no one to make the match too. Keeping my fingers crossed, we stepped in to the Raizada house. For our meeting was pre planned, the whole family for a change was present and received a warm welcome. The Raizadas talked to Dev and his mom while I slipped into Sruthy's room.

She was nervous and even then she looked gorgeous. I did mention to her about the meeting and informed Shishirji ji about Dev and his interest in Shruthy. It's after that he agreed to meet us.

The initial introduction went fine and Dev was allowed to have some private time with Sruthy. The elders discussed the proposal and a date for the wedding was decided to skip the engagement, as Dev's mom had brought a Kada (thick gold bangle given by the in laws to the would be daughter-in—law as a sign of accepting her in the family) and was gifted to Sruthy formally declaring her as a member of Dev's family. Both the families were excited and then came the snacks and sweets. It was during the time I sat with Mrs. Mrinali and told her the truth that her son wasn't married to Ankita. And Dev briefed the rest to the family with the evidence. All of sudden Sruthy hugged me and cried "Bhaabhi I told you he loved no one other than you . . . ."

The whole audience out there although family was stunned at the reaction. I myself couldn't respond in the best way and had to ask Sruthy to calm down and have some water.

Shishirji ji explained to Dev and his mom emotionally "If the untoward accident hadn't occurred Akruti would be here as our daughter in law. She is still a member of the family and it's her word I took to decide on Dev."

Should I say I was embarrassed? Soon the time to depart came and I asked Dev to take mom to the hotel while I'd return with Sruthy and would keep him posted. In a way I could get to know more about Rahul and Dev could spend some time with his mom.

No sooner had they left I thanked Raizadas for accepting my suggestion for having Dev as their son in law. Shruthy took me to her room and I'd to elaborate the photograph and the hidden truth behind it.

She was glad yet worried too as the truth came much too late.

I wanted to know more and this was the time . . . "Shrutz . . . tell me are you happy?"

"Yes a million times bhaabhi how can I repay you for this life you have gifted me?" she shivered.

"Cut the sentiments and I want your help to know more on what happened to your bhai . . . who's Ankita and where is she now ?What had happened ?Any info would be a help . . . so think hard and tell me."

"Well Bhaabi . . . we know Ankita since child hood days and her parents were well settled abroad. She was the only one who visited her maternal grandmother and ancestral home in Nagpur. She would come to Mumbai, stay here and then leave to Nagpur. Often bhai would take her by car. They used to be good friends. She is a doctor by profession. It was known that when bhai left to make his career he used to stay with her and they got married. These photographs were sent by bhai to us and he never talked about Ankita or the marriage to us and we never asked being furious at his decision. I did hate him too till the moment you told us he hadn't tied the knot. When things cooled down dad tried calling him and reached his friend. It's from him that we knew bhai is no longer staying with Ankita and that she has filed a divorce. We tried calling bhai several times but the last news wasn't late to reach us." she sobbed.

My phone vibrated "Lemme take the call must be Dev . . . hello . . . hello who's there?" I could see Sruthy blushing by the very name Dev. No one spoke on the phone and I'd to end the call. This happened often." Must be some disturbance in connection. "Yes tell me. And what did you get to know from his friends?" I enquired his friends.

"They said about their sky diving adventure and that they never knew where bhai had fallen after the parachute failed to open."

"Is there anything more you have to tell me? Well, I will be leaving for UK in a week's time for an assignment. It might take a couple of months or even a year to be back. Aditi is engaged now and mom will be with her brother in village until I return. I will keep in touch with you and Gracy. Even if I can't make it to your wedding trust me my wishes and prayers will be with you for ever. Think . . . is there anything you want me to know?" I knew these would perhaps be the final words before a long break.

"Only one thing . . . You will always be my bhabhi and come back soon". She said as she hugged me.

I bid her farewell, sought blessings from Shishirji ji and Mrs. Mrinali who this time held my palm tight to her heart and wished me luck. "You hold a special place in my heart though I haven't told you. Take care my child" she fled to her room.

Before the scene could get worse I left for the hotel. Took a cab for a change as I felt asking Sruthy to drop me would be awkward if Dev's mom wouldn't like that. She is of an orthodox mind, better compared to his dad.

Reached the hotel. Dev was waiting the lobby. Said I would meet him for dinner after I freshen up.

At 8pm we met at the Oregano Snacketeria.

He was alone.

"Hey there mom's tired and had her dinner ordered to the room. She has an early morning flight. Will drop her at the airport by the time you get busy with our return schedule. I'd called Sruthy. Glad she isn't nervous any more and she sounded upset on your trip to UK. Had to explain to her that you required a vacation and something to keep you away from the past and she agreed. Any news from her side on Rahul?"

"Rahul? Nothin particular Dev. He's gone and there's nothing I can do about other than tear my heart into pieces. I know I still love him and miss him but . . . I don't know". My head sunk. "I am happy I was able to see so many happy faces before I leave. But for a last time I would want to talk to Ankita."

"Why Ankita . . . ?"Dev paused.

"She was the last one to be associated to Rahul abroad. May be she has a different version to his disappearance."

CHAPTER 13

Love is a mirage

Time waxed and day gave way to night; yet he lay where he was . . . soon he had slept.

The door bell rang. He ran to fetch the door. She was at the door . . . . he couldn't resist him self and kissed her at once and wouldn't let her go. She hugged him tight and embraced him. He felt like a child at her arms. She put his head on her lap and wept. He wept till all his sorrows no longer existed. He kissed her fingers, hands, her face, sliding to her neck and her supple protrusions. Sliding his hands wildly over her waist and navel and back. She never spoke nor resisted yet her eyes spoke, she was willing and so was he. Only she could contain the beast within him, his love that could break all odds between them. He felt himself safe in her and could feel himself wildly ravaging and tearing her apart till she moaned. Each time she pushed him he grabbed her and clung to her biting her flesh like a wild boar.

This time she is all mine and I won't let her go this time.

She cried and he held her tight. She was pale and lifeless. He kissed her. He felt he was loved for very first time and the thought he had his love with him, all for himself and forever could make him a winner. But why did his lips bleed?

"Boss . . . boss . . . are you alright . . . boss . . . please open your eyes . . ." he faintly heard a familiar voice and in no time the voice increased. He opened his eyes to see Jane glare at him. He felt weak and was on the floor.

Jane helped him stand and slowly took him to the couch. "What happened and how come you are here?" he asked Jane.

"I was here to pick you to office. Had tried your phone but there was no answer. The calling bell wasn't answered hence I'd to open the door with the spare keys to make sure you are fine. Sorry for breaking in boss. But your lips . . . its hurt."

She made him breakfast and soon he was off to office with her.

This was the first time he felt so much relieved and the day seemed to giving him hopes of a better life. He smiled.

Soon after the meetings Jane commented "You look different boss. Hope everything's fine."

"It is and will be . . . Thanks Janet", he smiled at her and that would have been the very first time Jane had seen him so. She couldn't believe what she had just seen. Had he? Yes he did . . . not being sure of herself and unable to trust her own eyes she mumbled.

Ricky took his usual place in the study and this time all his correspondence ended on a cheerful note. The effect had spread and the results were evident that Ricky had changed and Jane had to answer all the queries on the new approach meant to all the clients and the contacts that had been mailing Ricky for years now.

Jane had nothing to say but she was happy for the man she adored and was devoted to have turned into a mortal from a beast. This could definitely bring greater glory to his life and the lives around him too. She was sure the secret behind this change was definitely the large portrait in his secret room. Jane was the only one other than him to be to the room. One day she will be honored to know about the lady with mysterious smile who could give life to a stone, her boss.

CHAPTER 14

In search of life

"A better life is what anyone in the world expect. There aren't exceptions to it if you are formed of flesh and blood. And I'm no exception. I need a change and live better". She felt lighter. So did the world . . . it seemed different. A sense of acceptance and a ray of hope washed away her worries.

"I will choose my life and doing justice to the love I'd for Rahul I will seek the truth". She thought as she shook Dev vigorously.

"Dev . . . Dev don't you think I deserve a better life . . . a good one, a happier one?"

"Sure you do and why such a question now? Dev queered at me.

"Just like that Dev . . . Let's go".

The trip back home filled my mind with fresh expectations. I'd started wishing and for no reason my mind had set to take the trip as a journey that could change my life for good.

Home seemed to be far than any time before. I wanted to be with mom and Aditi. This could have been earlier. Better late than never. Mom had been waiting for my return. How many times she would have waited for me and they always went unnoticed?

Aditi had grown without much care from my side. Though I cannot compensate their love; I wish I can give them love I had not been able to.

Mom was not at the door as I'd expected. "Mom . . . I'm back where are you? Too many news for you . . ."

Mom wiped her wet hands on her sari pallu and rushed towards me . . . "I was waiting for you at the door then thought you'd like garma garam samosa, so am done with that too. Come. Let me get you something to eat."

Aditi . . . . Aditi . . . . Kruti's home . . . come down or else we aren't leaving any samosas for you . . . first come first serve . . ." she chuckled.

This is the first time after dad left us I've seen her laugh. She happy for Aditi and asking her to find a pair for me would have given her some peace of mind.

After the tummy treat we got ourselves ready to go to the beach. It was my idea. Thought we could spend some time together. The rickshaw ride left us bit shaky. It had covered all the gutters and humps. The beach was unusually calm and being off season the beach seemed clear without much crowd.

Mom and I made ourselves comfortable on the sand while Aditi kept herself busy chasing the waves. "You know how much I had wished to see you happy? From the day you came to this world, you were a gift to us and all we wished for was to fill your life with all joy we could afford. But . . . ." mom paused.

"But what mom? I'm happy and it's purely because you were there for me always. I can't dare to imagine a world without you all?"

"Why did God give you so much in your life? My little girl had seen the worst days even I fear . . . I mean why you?" mom was low.

"But see He has given the strength to overcome all of it too na maa . . . so don't worry. Everything's gonna be just fine". I tried to change the mood.

Aditi seemed crazy. She still is a kid. I still remember we used to spend most of our time in the beach after school. And when Gracy came in we'd have a blast at the beach. Food packets were a must and long hours of chit-chat. Rahul and I almost spent days here when we were not at college. The sea used to talk to us and for everyone else they were mere voices but we could hear them loud and each day there used to be a new story.

The last vacation perhaps. I am never sure when I'll be back.

"Mom c'mon . . .", I pulled her with all might and in no time we were in water jumping and splashing water at each other like crazy kids.

Time flew and the sea seemed roaring at us and chasing us out of the beach. Took a walk back and the way home, had some snackie from the roadside dhaba. They make great 'vadas' and cool 'gilli tanda'. I wonder what the recipe is. All happens so fast you hardly get to see what all they add.

CHAPTER 15

Farewell Anmod

Just two days to the journey. Have lots more to do. Skipping breakfast wasn't difficult. Called up Gracy on the way and said I'd be dropping in for a brekfast. Reached Gracy on time and this time Gracy was pink and chubby. She had put on weight after our last visit. She had a noticeable bump too. The pregnancy showed and she looked beautiful.

We did share couple of hours and bidding farewell to the best friend who stood by me at all odd and awkward and some of the best times ever, I pushed off to meet Dev, the man who had given me a second chance to live. Dev had called me at morning saying he would have the last session of the therapy, a formal conclusion of it and God knows what he had in store for me.

This time of the year the blossoms are all wavy. This place is a heaven . . . I mean Dev's cottage. It takes you to a secretive den and there's lot much to experience nature to mind sync. And Dev is a true mediator in the sense.

11 am, Tuesday

Dev was at this therapy room. This is the very first time I've seen him treat someone. He is a good listener, but how does he find the solution to all the problems crazy nuts have? I'm no exception. Dev smiled and his eyes rolled from one end to another making a great curve . . . and I guess it meant just be at the living room . . . . I accepted the gesture with a smile and let the therapy continue.

Had some time before my therapy starts hence thought to take a peek-a-thon at Dev's cottage. I never ventured beyond the living room if not the therapy room. The house was neatly furnished and had strong fragrance of incense. There are three rooms in total. Two facing each other and the third at the end of a long corridor. They had colored doors too. Shades of purple, green and ivory.

"What in the world am I doing?? Peeking at private rooms . . ." my inner conscience pulled me back. Putting the silly mind to take a break I peeked at the rooms with purple and green doors. They were plain and had no furnishing at all except for thin curtains.

I wanted to stop myself from entering the third room but my curious feet wouldn't listen and in a moment I was at the door . . . and the next second in. The room had great design much sophisticated for Dev's brain. The shades were attractive and the furniture apt. A neatly made high bed, large dressing and array of cabins that neatly sat next to the dressing.

"Hey there . . . how did you like it?" Dev gave me a shock . . . Ashamed at my stupid curiosity; I tried to skip the question.

"Well are you done with the therapy . . . ?"

"Yes and tell me did you like the room? I had it done for Sruthy . . . any alterations required? I'm always open to suggestions . . ." he took me to the gazebo that stood few steps outside the master bedroom.

"Its great and I approve both. Your taste and the love for Sruthy. She's a lucky one . . . but dare not bring tears in the wide beautiful eyes of my little girl . . ." I warned him for which he swore crossing his heart . . .

"Arey . . . Ramcharan coffee to lao . . ." he yelled at the old man at home. He never talked to me. Must be fearing the psycho in me . . . and occasionally I enjoyed giving him weird looks and nasty stare.

Coffee break ended when I was done with the plans for the journey and he popped . . . "Where have you arranged the stay?"

"Well . . . I haven't done that. Will have to find out from the Mission Office." I confessed my poor planning technique.

"Alright then, I will give you Tiara's number. She's Tara my, first cousin, has well settled in Burlington. You may stay with her. She does have a guest room or portion whatever and would be happy to have you there. Did get it confirmed for you at morning."

He passed on the contact details and then we headed to the therapy room. This time the therapy was simple questions to know what I'd decided to do with my life and must have given him a tough time. Discussing the wedding plans and the investigations I am to do, we decided to part with a hope to meet with good news.

Before I got into the car he gave just one warning . . . "She's Tiara dare not call her Tara and you will see yourself homeless dear . . ." and he waved.

"She'll meet you at the airport. Bon voyage"

Dev's face faded away from the rear view mirror before me and the next destination was obviously home. The thought of packing my stuff did bug me a lot. One that I'm a poor packer and second with each item I pack, I was leaving my home for long. Had a stop over at a super market to get the necessary goodies for the journey. Gladly mom and Aditi had begun the ceremonial packing job and I had to just checklist the requirements. The truth that moms are moms I could see home made snack packs and herbal stuff like sandal,turmeric,besan and oil had been neatly packed too. Had to put them back on the table nearby. I could see mom frown at what I'd done and had to explain her that food items and liquids are not allowed or else it would trouble my clearance at the UK airport.

"Ma . . . I'd be staying at Dev's cousin's place and here's the contact number in case of emergencies. I'll call you when ever possible. It'll take some time till I get to know the city and about the facilties.", and handed her a parchment containing Tara aka Tiara's number.

"Don't talk to strangers and make sure you get home cooked food only. Keep a knife under the pillow. That will keep you away from nightmares. I still wonder what is the need of going abroad. Can't you find any job here Kruti?"

I simply blinked at mom and she nodded her head in dismissal. "As soon as the packing is done, check the papers you have to keep in your purse and Virat will be here at morning to see you off. Let Aditi come with you. She can call me when you've checked in. Kruti I'm not happy that you are leaving but I have compromised my mind for your happiness. Come back soon for me."

"I know maa. I'll be back soon. I want you to be strong and take care of yourself."

Wednesday 5 am

I was up early this time cos it never happened usually. Rechecked the documents and was all set in an hour's time. Virat sprung from no where, its later I got to know that Virat had been home yesterday night itself to avoid twice the distance and had made himself comfortable at the veranda. He was all fresh and full of jive. God . . . how do these men be so fresh without a proper sleep and are ever ready when it comes to putting their hands on the wheel?

Guys! They drive daily yet the craze for the car increases with each day.

The drive to the airport was quick and there was enough time to check in. Yet I bid adieu to the love birds and gave them their privacy. One the formalities were done and clearance over, I called up Virat to inform alls well.

"Virat, now Aditi and the whole family is your responsibility and promise me you will be there for them." I know it was a weird assurance yet I'd want you to do this for my inner peace.

"Don't worry Didi . . . I promise to tacare of mom and Aditi. Less than what you do cos no one can replace your love for them. And keepin touch as I'm a great guy and I do have enough contacts world wide who could be at your service on a call. Well forget the first part the second part is sure. You can call me for any help. Didi, I have couple of great friends to get you help on any issue. Have a great journey and we will be expecting your call. Cheers!!"

"Thanks for everything Virat you are a great guy . . . take care. Bye" . . . the call ended.

Hope the journey will be great. I found myself a place at the waiting area. One hour spent and then a half. I couldn't bear waiting. The whole airport was in chaos. I could see a crazy little kid running into a book shop and lo he comes out but this time he was on the floor. His mom was pulling him all the way back to the seat. There were people at the coffee shop. They are there since the time I took the seat. "Are they having too much coffee or sipping the same coffee for more than an hour???" I wondered.

There were mobile phones ringing now and then. Some of them with usual ring tones and few with fundu "dinchak" sort of hip-hop tunes. All of them had to give their travelogue to the person at the other end. My eyes were burning and heavy. I felt sleepy and in this time I'd have peeked at my wrist watch for more than twenty times and my mobile more than ten I guess.

This is a small airport and the facilities were limited as the number of seats. Most of them never left their seats fearing they'd have to stand till they board the flight. My flight has a stop over at Dubai for an hour. I'd be dead if the status quo remains.

I must have cat napped for minutes and 'ding dong', the announcement for my flight came. I had to decipher what the voice said as it came as a muffle. Perhaps the lady would have a half eaten cake in her mouth when the mic was on for her voice to wake me up.

I boarded the flight, my heart sank and I was in mid air. I felt a pain within me and felt my heart is being torn into pieces. I missed mom and Aditi. I wanted to go home right away. Had to keep my eyes closed till I could gain the strength to convince my mind and tutor my heart that alls for good. Few hours must have passed and I could here coughs and conversations occassionally. Not giving any heed to the voices my senses had demanded to sleep and I followed them well.

At Dubai, nothing changed except some wheatish faces were replaced by whitish ones. I have no offence to the good souls from the Western part of the globe yet it did clearly show they were fair enough to over do our fairness creams and make up. I ordered my food in flight and munched on fiercely with no mercy. More hours to the destination. I listened to music and watched movies but couldn't take it after the number of movies exceeded two. I tried to sleep. The lady beside me had great looks but as the saying does looks can deceive. For rest of the journey, her snore turned out to be my lullaby.

Sooner or later I felt my tummy sinking and my legs numb. Slowly opening my eyes I could see the crew adding yet another bottle of perfume to their neat coat and the seat belt sign indicated it was time to touch down. Putting my self upright with great difficulty, I wiped my self fresh with the warm towel the crew had served. The warmth was refreshing after the icy cool trip.

Once the door opened all the passengers were in a frenzy to squeeze themselves out for the next set of clearance and to jump out of the airport. They looked more like little kids after the school bell rang. They had no idea where to move; yet they were out. I took my own time to admire the airport and the beautified shops within with any thing and everything in the world. They had great price tags too. Picking up the baggage wasn't an easy task. After the flight my body seemed swollen like fresh dry cotton and I found it really hard to carry myself to the exit.

CHAPTER 16

Home away from home

The climate was pleasant and I've heard it remains neutral unlike India where extremes are common and undue rainfalls are always added to the dues. The clearance was pretty quick. Thanks for the great brains behind sidelining the eatables and liquids. The airport was as I said, huge and more than a hundred flights took off and landed every second here. Hats off to the air traffic control, for their patience and presence of mind.

I wondered if Tiara would have arrived. If she hasn't turned up? What if she wouldn't turn up? What am I going to do next?

All sorts of negative thoughts found good enough space in my mind. As the saying goes . . . an idle mind is a devil's workshop. If true, my mind can be reasonably called Devil's palace or estate!!

Without much wait, I forced my trolley to pull me to the receiving area and my eyes searched for my own name. The last time I did this would be to see my examination results. They used to be good but what's gonna happen this time?

As I'd thought, Tiara had dumped me and I'm all alone to suffer the rest of my stay in never land.

I tried to be calm and this time the breathing exercise didn't help me. I tried to concentrate and closed my eyes and took a deep breath. "Hello . . . hope you haven't slept off . . ." a voice broke my breath in to a burst of carbon dioxide.

The lady waved her hand in thin air. I wonder if she wanted to check whether I'm blind or not.

"Hey there. How's your journey been? Dev had called me. Sorry the parking at the airport is a bit cranky. Run we got to reach home early. With no further introduction the lady grabbed me by my arm and took me to her car-a Bug. I'd to squeeze my self with the luggage and car rocketed at once.

The lady kept herself steady on wheels and checked the rear view mirror now and then. "By the way why do you have a strange look there? I haven't kidnapped you . . . darling!!! I'm Tiara . . . and you can call me Tiara.

I was for once relieved. The race had put lot of doubts which was cleared by a mere name. In 30 minutes, we reached the so called home sweet home. It looked in no way different from the rest of the houses in the lane. "How in the world would the people here find their home?" She unlocked the door and the green carpet led to a long corridor. She initiated the home viewing.

"Do you see this neat little room? This is my study room and this is not the room for you. C'mon the room to the right is the master bedroom and it is mine and for sure, it isn't yours either . . ." I was disturbed and tired.

"Tiara where would the room for me be. Hope it isn't too far . . . you see the bags are pretty heavy."

"Oh my oh my. That just skipped out of my mind. Hop on let me take you to your room."

She quickly skittered across the dining area and the massive kitchen. On the farther end of the kitchen was a door neatly decorated with a funny tag "Enter at your own risk!!"

The very sight of the board gave me mixed emotions and fear grappled me. But the fear vanished as the door flung open. The room was exclusive and starting from the paints to the furniture everything seemed perfect suit to my mood.

"I hope you like it. It was done as per Dev's orders and hope you will be comfortable here."

It was more like an independent apartment made for me and just for me. "Thanks Tiara. I see you have taken too much effort but this is great and I really have no words to thank you dear!"

"Take a chill pill and we will catch up @ dinner. Any thing just scream out for me . . ." and she simply vanished. "This lady is something . . . ." I said to myself.

The room had enough light and the view to the next street was a bonus. A little door led to the backyard and the little garden where roses of all colours stood. They seemed happy. Slowly the unpacking and storing began and in an hour I was done. A hot shower eased my body ache and lo my body was soon under the wraps. I couldn't be even more shameless. But the journey had left me worn out.

Amidst of my sweet beauty sleep, there where scrams and laughter. When they grew louder the bed was shaky and I was almost bounced out off the bed. To my astonishment two little kids, a boy and a girl . . . must be younger were gleefully jumping on my bed and screaming their life out. I felt myself in an asylum; put to test with a group of crazy baboons. They were here, there and everywhere.

Soon a mild knock and Tiara was in. Her eyes peered at the kids and they silently exit the room. In a fraction of second her face lit up and she apologized for the nasty behaviour. The room I was in, used to be their play area and they were yet to tame their mind too. She left me to continue my nap session.

The room seemed cool and dark. I could hear the crickets chitter. The time was 8 pm, I had tuned my watch to UK standard time from the very moment I was at airport. My body still ached. Gladly, I am to meet the boss only in a day's time. Have enough time to prepare physically and mentally, I thought. Slow but steady, I found my way to the dining area and Tiara was at the cleaning area. She laid a neat plate on the table and there came the spaghetti and fresh orange juice.

"I hope you don't mind the Italian. Here, in UK Indian food is costly the way Italian are in India so most of the time I cook Chinese, Italian or mostly the breads take the main course." She wiped her hand on the apron and sat beside me with a glass of juice.

"I understand you have gone through a lot and I'm sure the stay and work here will surely change your life. The people I must say are always busy and you need to make prior appointments even if you are at the verge of delivering a baby. No ones bothered what rest of the world do and expect the same from others too. You make your life here." Tiara started with the city life and ended in her family. Her husband, a banker by profession is a busy body and turns up pretty late from work. She says her day begins at night. They are awake all night and she's sure to be fine the next morning to be with the kids like any other cool mom.

She finds herself busy most of the time and has never thought of taking up a job thinking that would ruin the family life. She feared her kids would leave them in early teens, the way other kids did, if they are not attended well enough. And the cultural values being minimum abroad has added to her worries. After the dinner, she led me to my room and silently closed the door behind.

In a moment she was back "oops sorry Dev had called. I informed that you have safely reached and he's informed your mom about the same. You needn't worry. We will get a mobile number first thing in the morning. Goodnight and sleep tight."

As promised, as soon as the breakfast was done we were out. Dropped the kids at their school which is just a block away from home and then to the shopping wonderland. In addition to what I had, Tiara bought me few formal shirts, skirts and trousers saying that would help me keep myself in fashion. I agreed. "I hope my first pay won't burn out in the first shopping itself." I thought.

We had been out till lunch and munching a hotdog back home, we were done for the day's outing. I called mom and her voice cracked. Fearing the call would eat up all the balance it held, I made the call short and pacified her saying I'm fine and would call her after I'd taken up the assignment. I know she was sad but the more I talk to her the more I will be home sick. Tiara would have read my mind. She came up to me and said "C'mon mighty Indian lady, you are here with a mission to make something good of your life. You will be fine and don't hesitate to make calls from the landline here too." and smiled.

"Gracious" I said. That was the only word that could fit well in the scene. "I will try not to but if it troubles my mind I might as well make a call till my mind settles to work." I replied softly.

"No worries and formalities darling." She seemed too different a person I'd met at the airport yesterday. The Dev effect was evident and priority. At dinner, we were together. The kids Kris (Krishna) and Cherry (Chirag) were my best buddies after I'd allowed them to share the room and we did spend some good time in stories too.

Mr. Vardan (Harshvardan) joined us for dinner and he seemed to be a lovable husband despite his busy schedule. He offered me a lift to my office tomorrow and we retired to our respective rooms after the dinner.

7 am Saturday

I expected a holiday but most of the Brits worked on Saturdays to make up the days lost during the public holidays. Mr. Vardan dropped me at the office and wished me luck and before he left he said "Call me bhaiyya . . . that sounds better. I hate my name now, it used to be Harshvardan and here no one calls me by my own name. The fate is same for all Indians including kids. The good people here find it difficult to call Indian names. Hope you get a good name today. See you at dinner tonight. Well, you'll get a cab around the corner and just give 'em the street name and you will be dropped there. Cheers and good day!"

The office was a small one and there were only 10 staff including myself. I saw that most of the work was over the phone and computer. I met my boss.

Mr. Anderson was a tall hefty figure with gruff voice. He was pleasant and explained what my assignment was all about. It did contain field trips but initially the training sessions would be held at the office's conference hall with other team members who would assist me to get used to the project and its pattern. I felt sleepy. I guess the jet lag hadn't left me completely. From the next week onwards, I would be on board and 5 days of work with perks and salary. I get the transportation paid too. What more could you ask for? For the day, I was asked to go through the assignment framework and the guidelines. I was also introduced to the whole office including the pantry and the security room. Mine was a neat cubicle with well set stationary and a laptop for office use.

I made myself comfortable and was asked to leave early once I'm done with the reading; this being my first day. Each time I laid my eyes on the sheets that counted 12 in number, my eyes would shut automatically and I must have had a couple of coffee before I was done. Once the thing was over, I slipped out of the office and made my way to the corner of the street and Bhaiyya was indeed a genius. I got a cab and was home in no time. First thing I did was to call mom. She was much relieved after I told her how Dev and Tiara had made for me a new home and the first day at office. Conveying my regards to Aditi, I went to the next one in the list; Dev, Gracy and Sruthy. Calls were done and I retired to the room when Tiara had already set neat snack on my table with a note that she won't be back until 3 pm and I could take rest till she back. The note also said she would wake me up when she's home to continue chit-chat. This time I was all into it cos I'd started liking her character and she is indeed a warm person and a great chatter.

The snack was a square meal and I made the best use of time by taking a short nap. Tiara was back on time as promised. To be a better inmate, I'd fixed the tea and put some assorted cookies which I'd seen in a neat jar. Kids were home and before any word came in they were all munching the cookies. Tiara gestured the kids to have their fun time at the garden behind and they proved too obedient in this issue.

The initial discussions were of the first day at office and then the school reports. Slowly when we were left with nothing much to discuss, Tiara put up her next question . . .

"So Akruti, what are your plans with the past relationship? Dev had said you would want to meet some people, his friends and get to know more . . . tell me dear why in the world do you want to dig the past? Don't you think it's high time to move on? I mean . . . I didn't want to interfere in your issues but just a concern." She shrugged.

"Well . . . you are right at that Tiara; the issue is past but even before we know each other well, the concern that provoked you ask this question is the same reason that forces me to find what has been done to Rahul. The only difference being that you know me less and I know him more than anyone in this whole wide world." and I smiled.

"You got it baby. I'm in. What ever is required be sure I'm with you in this trail", she gave me a high five.

In no time she made the whole plan sound adventurous and felt I'd gained an advantage against fate that left me with a million question that need to be solved through well-knit puzzles.

"Tiara, one more point . . . may I pick and drop the kids from school, just because I get bored all the way to my office. Any time I will be stuck then I'll let you know well in time and you can be the super mom."

In seconds her face lit up . . . and she responded in a heavy voice . . . "Oh my how in the world would I thank you. How much I wished for a spare time for myself to make sure I don't ignore myself. This is going to be great. Are you sure it won't be a trouble???" she seemed to cross check.

"Perfectly fine with me", I assured. She gave me a tight hug and ran to her kids to share the bit of news she had got. Soon all three were jumping up and down Tiara too seemed to be one among them. She was still a child at heart.

I knew I had to prepare myself for the new responsibility but there was still a day left to take charge. But Rahul . . . the weekend is the time I could spare.

CHAPTER 17

Hunt the past to find the present

6 am Sunday

Unlike other weekends, I was up early. The thought I am on a mission to solve a puzzle filled my senses and in no time, I was on. But where do I begin. To make sure the track was right I'd to put my plans in black and white. It did get some cuts and edits but I was clear what I'd to do next.

First thing in the morning, I got myself a Yellow pages directory and tried my fingers to get Dr. Ankita. It was a tough call. There was no one by that name. Atleast no doctor.

"The first attempt itself a failure . . . think think think . . ." I could feel the pencil tip resting comfortable on my forehead. Sruthy's face appeared in my mind . . . it was a sign. I called up Sruthy at once.

The phone bell rang and I wonder why each time the call to Raizadas left my heart thumping faster than I could handle. Sruthy was at the other end.

"Sruthy Akruti here. Have you got the contact number for Rahul's friends in UK or else where? Any one? And any number for Ankita? I need them ASAP", I was all ears for her.

"Bhabhi . . . I see that you have settled well. Hold on a moment "and she passed on few numbers she had, one of Jain in UK and the rest in U.S.A

"Nothing about Ankita. Why don't you try Dev.? He may be able to help you". After a pleasant chat I was on call with Dev and he assured to get back to me with the details in an hour or two.

I left at home a note for Tiara that I am on the trail and will let her know when she has to enter the case soon. From the public booth, I tried Jain's number and in a minute, a squeaky voice answered. He must have tried mock the British accent but poor it didn't work the way he wanted.

"Mr. Jain, my name's Akruti and I'm . . . I'm a friend of Rahul Raizada. I would like to talk to you in this regard."

"Oh . . . that's fine can you make it to the Winter Park in an hours time. I will be there". He ended the call

Now how am I going to know who's Jain. I could have asked him for some way to identify him. My state of mind didn't allow me to make a second call and I was on a cab to the so called Winter Park.

The lush greenery soothed my mind and waiting for Jain seemed no trouble for me if this peace would remain longer. There was greenery everywhere and the dew drops dangling from the tip of leaves shone bright and was a sure delight to the eyes.

A dew drop fell on the forehead and that made a slight reflex where in the eyebrows took a sharp curve and relaxed again. I ran my fingers through his hair, smooth and shiny that kept falling over his cute little eye brows. He seemed sleeping like a baby with nothing but peace. Neither were there lines of worry nor shades of distress.

I found my whole world evolve around this face that shone bright and gave me hopes on which I could push a life time. Nature was the only companion we had. Hours would pass talking about our life together and even the trees would sway to support us. The winds would flow with fragrance and his eyes that held a million secrets would shine. I could see seamless joy and dreams in them. I would lean on his shoulder with nothing but belief that our dreams would be a reality someday and reading my mind he would gently rest his cheek over my head.

I loved Rahul . . . he was my life.

The vibration of the phone gave me a jerk. "Dev's call . . . must be some piece of news . . . Hello Dev . . . Akruti here . . . what have you got for me?"

"You're one lucky soul. Take down Ankita's address. She stays just few blocks off Tiara's. The clinic she owned is no longer active yet she does some private consultation at home. Good luck and do take care. Alls well here."

"Dev, take care" I replied. He wouldn't have accepted a thanks. Formality to him is a sin and I would never want to be a sinner in his view.

"I know you Kruti. Keep me posted and remember you are a great lady. Call me when you need a friend." His voice never seemed so soothing and sure.

The wait was over as I could see a plum yet tall person roaming in the park with no intention other than hunting a lost puppy dog. I walked to him hesitantly and saw him murmuring something. My ears had to be sharpened.

"Akruti . . . Akru . . ." the voice was feeble yet squeaky.

"Excuse me. Are you Mr. Jain? And there was a vigorous nod.

The intro faded quickly and we found a comfortable bench to talk. I felt I was in an interview all set to grill him.

"Mr. Jain, as I said anything you know about Rahul, any thing at all after her arrived here in UK. Any contacts any thing . . ." instead of reply he kept staring at me.

"You . . . I've seen you somewhere. It is clear . . . we talked about you. We . . . . yes the snap in Rahul's wallet. That's you right? You . . . you're Rahul's wife aren't you . . . and you say you are a friend of his. Tell me what you want?" he turned aggressive.

"Calm down Mr. Jain . . . please . . . let me explain. We were engaged but never married. If Rahul had said so to you it was out of nothing but his love for me. If you could spare me few minutes I'd explain." he took his place on the bench and I shared with him what I had been carrying in my mind and what I was seeking.

"I'm sorry if I'd hurt you and I'm happy that you have seen me worthy of your cause. Well, Rahul and I'd been together in college and being his senior we had limited our contacts to college and when it was time to leave I' given him my email contacts to keep in touch. In a years time, I was placed here in UK and the mail stating that Rahul was here came as a surprise, All I wanted and did was get all our buddies together and have some old time rewound with remixes", he laughed.

"We used to go to pubs and movies and had some good trips too. Rahul, I can say is the best person I've seen a great friend, a good thinker and a true sportsman. If only he hadn't put himself in issues with that . . . Ankita. He lost the faith of his family and their tears must have drowned him. He never met us after that and kept himself busy in holidays and work. A workaholic, which was a swift transformation. We did talk after that and he seemed fine when he was about to leave for his Europe tour with Damian and his expedition group. Damian, our common friend here works with a Travel and Holiday Planner, the Carla Tours and Travels. I can get him to meet you and can give you his contact too.

If you could excuse me for a moment, he placed a call which ended in a minute and he returned to me with a swollen face. "Miss Akruti, Damian will be meeting you at evening after he calls you. All he says is he knows nothing of what happened to Rahul after they had dived from the aircraft.

"I understand Mr. Jain. You may ask him to cancel the meeting. He may be right. By any chance Mr. Jain, do you think Rahul could have survived the fall? My hands froze yet my head burned.

"God be with you". He patted my shoulder and led me to the cab. I could see the meeting end there.

Back home Tiara was all set to hear what I'd for her. The long story took a short form and I retired to the room. Some sort of exhaustion had gripped me tight. I found my self pasted on to the table with my head resting on my arms. Knowing this wouldn't yield me any solace, I emptied my pockets and a parchment slipped on its way to the table top. Picking the piece of paper was too much a task yet I'd to when I read the name Ankita. Placing the address safe in my diary, I slid myself under the blanket.

In minutes Tiara turned up. As usual the glass of juice had found its place on my bedside.

"Akruti, you must have had a hard day. Get some rest and when you are fine we shall talk". She held my palm tight. Before she left I pulled her back and she sat beside me. I could no longer swallow my grief and it was evident I found her lap as a pacifier. I felt childish but I couldn't hold myself. The grief had eaten my heart and my soul wandered aimless. My thought never sought a stand and my eyes were always searching for someone. I've to let go my life and stay strangled by the memories forever.

Tiara put me on the bed comfortably and moving away she made a call.

"Dev, Tara . . . I think Akruti has lost it. She's down and her hand are frozen. She's sweating and has weak pulse. Yes, I can do that. But I wish you were here. That will be great. Sure will do." I could hear her loud but each time I tried to call out that I'm fine no sound came out. I'm down? Where? I'm conscious but I felt I'm dead or rather half asleep. My eye lids weighed heavier than me and the last picture of Tiara was getting a pill from my drawer. She seemed to have vanished leaving just a white light.

CHAPTER 18

Lost love is life lost

Virat had been busy at his journal desk and this time his photos were more on sky diving and the accidents related. He had tried to help Kruti to get her search of facts done with his help. From the very day she left Aditi and Virat had been browsing for all news piece and images on Sky diving.

"I wonder what this really meant . . . it's been disturbing me for too long now. Wish I were more literate to get the surety to my thought." Virat sounded disturbed. Quickly Aditi slid her chair towards him to see what made her beau pass such a comment.

"What's it tell me. I can put my IQ on test once in a while? It won't hurt . . . for sure." Aditi winked.

Without hesitance, Virat extended a paper clipping to Aditi which read of the sky diving team that has missed a member during the adventure ending with failed attempts to recover the member's corpse. Aditi's face towards Virat had raised eyebrows and blank expressions. She read the news twice and more until she added to Virat's comment.

"Now I think I'm illiterate", they burst into laughter and Virat slowly changed the atmosphere into a serious one.

"Aditi the piece that says the corpse was not found . . . can't it mean there wasn't any corpse at all?"

"What does that mean an inexistent corpse?"

"No Miss Ant brain, it can mean that the person could be alive. I better check with the journalist and get more details". He scrolled through the contact list on his laptop and sent a mail. Rest of the hours were tense and anxiety built bundles of emotions unnamed.

11 pm Paris

The view of the well lit Eiffel tower was lovers delight but what it can mean to those whom love never favored nor did the luck? Such thoughts can come out of the deserted minds that yearned for nothing but love that could quench the thirst of life, giving it a complete meaning worth living.

Yet when mind does make a turn to go on, we tend to chose the destiny and blame on fate.

Ricky was occupied. Rather, his mind was and his eyes fixed on one of the greatest piece of art dedicated to one magic accepted by the universe and adored by human race. Paris is lovers' paradise and truly love fills the air. Ricky is no exception. The coffee cup half full and the laptop blinking with "New Messages" icon showed he was at work. His annual meeting gave him a chance to visit the 'Must see' locations and this time Paris. All alone in his suite room he maintained solitude.

The phone in his palm dialed the same number for the 25th time in three hours yet yielded the same results to recheck the number. This time he seemed desperate and his patience had died. He couldn't wait any longer and Jane was the only contact he could make.

"Jane, try the number I send. If you don't get through trace the id of the number." he commanded.

He threw the phone on the bed and sat hands on head in despair. Getting the in-house medic to sedate him with mild medications he was sound asleep.

Virat's inbox squeaked informing the new message update and in minutes a call was connected to Akruti. Yielding no response he tried again and this time Tiara was on the line.

"Diid . . . Virat here guess what we have fresh clicks"

"I'm afraid Akruti can take you call now, this is Tiara. How may I help you? Can I take down any messages?" Tiara answered courteously.

"Didi!!!! Is she alright?" listening to Virat's conversation Aditi snatched the phone from him at once. "Hi, this is Aditi, Akruti's sister. Where's Kruti and why is she not responding the call?"

Tiara explained what had happened. "Akruti had been unconscious for the past 24 hours and the Para medics were brought in to her help. They have done the needful and wait is the only option left. She's had a nervous breakdown due to stress." Tiara confessed.

"But . . . but how what stress. She yet to join her assignment".

"Yes, I have informed her chief and he's advised few days off. She'll be fine. Just that she has to take good rest and keep a clear mind. She had been trying to . . . you know . . . meet up with those Rahul knew. Perhaps something has hurt her. Stay calm. Will get back to you when she's fine to talk", Tiara comforted Aditi.

"Tiara, send me your mail id, I need you to check it immediately and please read the last note on Kruti diis diary. You will know what has hurt her. Don't hesitate. It has to be done to save her"

Tiara shared her id and moved to the Aditi's desk. She checked her Blackberry and viewed the message sent by Aditi. The diary was an easy pick right on the table. She at once ran through the pages and the parchment found its way out.

"Ankita, doctor? Now what's with the address?" She text messaged the details on the diary and Aditi responded on the details stating Ankita's role in the case.

Tiara was close to be involved herself in the mad hunt. She called up Dev who was on his way to meet her. Giving an update on Akruti and the recent data collected, she sat beside Akruti holding her palm. They were warmer. Tiara took a warm towel and wiped Akruti's face. Her eyes shrunk and her palm tightened over Tiara's.

Tiara slowly moved towards Akruti and slowly patted her cheeks . . . "Wake up little girl . . . you have been sleeping for too long wake up!"

Akruti flexed her muscles and tried to regain herself but the weakness had taken on and she was still. Her palm tightened and Tiara had to call Dev to make sure the medic wasn't required.

Dev warned Tiara not to disturb Akruti saying any force can make things tougher and to be with Akruti until the IV fluids is done. He was just hours from helping his good friend.

"Now how do we let Diid know that there no confirmed reports on the death of Rahul? She has to come back to get to the next level" Virat commented looking at the mail he'd kept active on the screen.

"Let's wait till she's fine Virat. I really don't want Kruti di to compromise her life for a man no where"

CHAPTER 19

Love if true . . . set it free.
If true, it shall find you

Bzzzzzzzz . . . The phone buzzed at Ricky's bed. Jane had left 3 missed calls. Ricky at once returned the call.

"Yes Jane the update first . . ." Ricky shot the response at once.

"The id could be traced but the holder can't be traced. So for now, the contact isn't possible. Is there any thing I can do for you? Regarding the office you need to get back to do the deal with Mathias as agreed." Jane hasted.

"Get the travel arrangements done and mail me. I'm done with the conference here."

Ricky felt he had lost the power to carryon his life. His faith had subsided. "What next?" was the only line that lingered his thought.

His life had been wound around her. Thought was not the right step. He stepped out of the hotel.

The winds were hard and every time he breathed he could feel the pain that emerged from his nostrils which traveled to his throat.

He could feel her at every step he took. She would hold him tight when ever the winds blew. He missed her and missed her so much that even hallucination could take him over yet he never resisted. She was everywhere he saw. The way he felt when he was with her.

He was formless and incomplete without her. May it be her thought or even the dreams. Before they fell for each other, how much he found it difficult to be near her without staring her even once. She would enchant him each time. Every day whatever he does, she could leave him spellbound looking at vaccum. Any chance to speak out his mind would vanish the moment her eyes met his and once she passes by, the result is a lost chance.

A love worth living and losing life for. All his dreams and thought had meaning when it was with her. Life and future meant more when she was with him. There were reasons for any thing he did, even meaningless acts would seem full of sense. It was easy to wake up early and wait at the street where she boarded the bus to college and follow her all the way. How stupid to follow someone with out an idea of what she had in her mind? Indifference was a sure response. How can I change the status quo?

The feelings undescribed that arouse from the depth of heart and spread to the whole body controlled the senses. He remembered the day he waited for her at the mall and there she came and his heart traveled to her at once. For one glimpse of her he could wait for hours. She neared him and with every step she took towards him, he would fill her in his eyes and mind. As she passed by, her hair, the aroma and the silky feel it left on his finger tips . . . God, he could die then and there . . . . if only she could be his. He could build the paradise for her and love her more than anything in the world. He believed fairy tales could be true if there were princesses like her and if a charm like hers existed.

He has to find himself a life and with some one who could keep him away from his past and be with him throughout. Jane . . . could have the answer. She knew everything about him and could find someone for him . . . "wait but why not Janet herself?" She is good and intelligent, supportive and considerate. "I will have to talk to her about it." This was the only way to be alive. "Live for someone if it's not for you." He made up his mind and mailed to Jane at her personal mail saying he would like to pursue his life with someone who would stand by him at all times and asked Janet's view on the same. He would be able to read her mind from the reply.

"I know it's a hasty decision but something need to be done to my life", Ricky said to himself.

At Tiara's, Dev had just entered. Throwing his luggage on the couch he hasted towards Akruti. She was pale; yet calm. The IV fluids were done and Tiara was beside her as he had advised.

"Any response?" Dev enquired and received a nod from Tiara indicating a "no"

He checked for her pulse and her pupil. She seemed normal but weak. He slowly sprinkled water on her eyes and called out her name.

"Kruti . . . its me Dev. Look at me I'm all the way here for you. You got to listen to me and wake up. We got lots of things to fix. Wake up slowly . . .".It did take few attempts yet never failed. She woke up from her long sleep and with all energy she could save, hugged him.

Tiara smiled and thought the privacy has to be maintained and left the room.

Dev joined her few minutes later.

"How's she Dev? Hope she will be fine soon." Tiara had to clear her doubts before she could proceed with her mind.

"Why don't you give her a life Dev? I see that you guys are so much in love yaar . . . then what's with the dead man walking?"

Dev pulled Tiara to meet Akruti and in the room, the lady who was so much bed ridden now had a smile on her face and she was surely alive.

Dev put the topic before Kruti that Tiara had popped few minutes back. That lightened the mood and both were all smiles. Dev took his place at the study table and told Tiara . . . "I'm engaged Tara . . . the girl is Sruthy . . . the so called Rahul's sister and it was Kruti who helped us out with turning this mess we had in our mind to a proper relation".

"Ok . . . Ok . . . I just felt you guys were cool with each other and don't call me Tara", she snorted.

"Come here Tiara. Did I scare you?" Kruti asked Tiara who sat beside her.

"This was a passing phase but I think too much of stress could still leave me dumb. I know you were beside me always yet I couldn't respond. Dev is not only my best friend, he's my therapist too and knows how to handle my breakdowns."

"I must admit you scared me but I was sure you will be back for we have great things to do. Remember the pick up and drop of the kids? You ought to keep the promise. Now take some rest. I will be back with some think to drink. Dev would you mind joining me?"

Tiara took her trip to kitchen followed by Dev.

Fixing him a coffee and a soup for Akruti was a simple multi tasking for Tiara. "What's wrong with her Dev?" Tiara had to clear her mind.

"She's fine except for her mind. See Tara, there are people who have emotions and we tend to juggle with emotions mostly to keep our mental balance. There are a few like Kruti, where their emotions control their minds. Therapy can work but only to a certain extent. Too much of turmoil with mind can create a crash like what Kruti had. She's is still in love baby . . ."

"But De . . . the girl must be crazy, if she goes on with her life like this she will be a psycho" she shot back.

"There are certain things you need to leave to destiny. Kruti isn't and never will be a psycho but I must admit from what I've learnt there is still a thin line of telepathy or some wave that links her to Rahul and after your call and the message you forwarded, I had a word with Virat and there are chances that this guy is not dead. I say not dead cos I'm least sure he would be alive after the fall."

"Anyways, I will be out to meet Ankita for Kruti, that's what my agenda holds. This time I'm with her till she pleads and excuses herself from the trail." Dev affirmed.

CHAPTER 20

Time heals wounds

In the dim apartment at Westmont, the cupid had struck late but right. Jane seemed immersed in thoughts along with the rising level of water in her bath tub.

Ricky has a change? What in the world would have happened and why me? Does he really want an "I do" or the hormones wanted a source to appease the wilderness in him? I want time and want him all for myself and this is the only chance I may get.

Janet adorned her self with a white satin gown and admired herself before the mirror. In mid-thirties, she has kept her figure intact and every inch and curve of her own body toned to grab the first glance of any man she could have wished for but wrapping herself in the business suit, she seemed to have wrapped her emotions along. Knowing the man she had eyed for years has finally given in to her, she was busy re-arranging her wardrobe pushing off the suits to give enough space to more seductive designer wear by Rosette Valpour.

Well in time the message bar blinked . . . DINNER AT 8 PM. MEET YOU AT BOURGES. Undoubtedly from Ricky. The time already 5 p.m. and there's hardly enough time to make sure she had enough to seize the heart of the beast. Perhaps the dinner is a date and more . . . Thoughts climbed heights. The choice was easy.

The puzzle was evident and was purposely framed. There were enough photos at Ankita's and the album was more a mini library neatly arranged with tons of them having Rahul as the only relative to the bride. Then why did he have to send the snaps that could create confusions and why did he never bother to clear any of them just letting the ties break with no reasons? It was not a mistake but pre-planned and well crafted project.

"Ankita, I would never want to intrude your private life but what is Rahul's role in your life?" Dev had to get the cues right this time to be of some help to Kruti.

From the conversation that lasted for couple of hours it was understood and with great care Dev jotted down the details he had in his note.

Rahul is Ankita's chuddy buddy and despite the strong disagreement from Ankita's parents, Rahul helped her get her life with Preet a reality. A normal by looks he was a bit psychic to have thought the dame had her yes and the whole body over the hero of our story, Rahul as a result of which he had been spying on her with his pair of eyes and extras with a private investigator PI do his job on his wife. Thank God he didn't suspect the PI to have an affair with his wife. The usual and casual relation ship ends with the guy absconding with the lady's fortune and the lady has good riddance not even bothering to complain robbery.

"Well, then why didn't you go ahead and file a case with the cops? His prank would have wiped your earnings. Being a doctor myself I believe you would have lost a hefty green bundle." Dev sympathized the damsel in distress.

"Believe me, I did and more than what you could expect. I let it go to avoid any chance to meet the bastard may it be even court. I have my parents visit me regularly now after the mishap. But Rahul. He'd nothing to do with this mess and got himself lost.

The date @ Bourges

The thought whether to say she liked Ricky and their decision to talk and learn about each other excited Jane.

Flaunting herself in the emerald green evening gown, Jane made her entry at the Bourges. The gown though vintage, had draped her tightly giving her figure the best display and the low neck could with less effort highlight her cleavage that safely rest beneath the diamond necklace that clung to her thin yet carved neck. She found her man sit all set to give her the most expected dinner that could make her life.

Ricky, dressed himself in a neatly tailored suit, had ordered himself a drink to hide his fear. The ambience of Bourges gave him shivers. They had dim lighting and all tables had just candle light. Though the path was lit the eeriness couldn't be exclaimed romantic.

I love her. She has made her life and I have to move on. Jane will help me move on. She loves me, or at least I believe she does. I know I'm not ready to tie the knot but some commitment would change the status quo. I'm not sure. Am I right? What if I'm doing a bigger mistake but pulling some one like Jane into a horrible life? She will be forced to suffer a miserable life with me.

After the first course, Ricky opened up.

"Jane, I know all this happened too fast for both of us but to make sure we are right I need you to know me better. And let me know more about you too."

Sleep with me you stud, I'll let you know me more than anyone does. Jane's mind howled.

"Yes, you are right Ricky. May I call you so?" Jane blushed.

"What ever you feel is right. Well, I'm done with the food. I've kinda lost my appetite recently" Ricky confessed.

"See you tomorrow at office on time" he added

Before they left Borges for the parking, she leaned forward to kiss him. That would have confirmed a date but before he could get the gesture loaded to his memory packed brains . . . he was gone.

The perfect geek. I wonder I have a mistake on the way. Good he needs time. I really think I need time to see he's good enough for me. High time I get Choco filled cream softies. Jane murmured.

She drove past the Bourges with hopes to come back for a better date with her sturdy boss.

Ricky was out for a walk. The thought of getting committed had filed his mind. This was something new but the very feel of getting bonded or rather detached from his past ached from inside.

How in the world can I know if she is alive and happy? Would she have died with a broken heart? I gave her hopes and dreams. She trusted me and I estranged her. She would have survived the tragedy and would have sought a better life. She would have pretty children. Girls with same fair complexion and wide eyes like hers or naughty boys like me or both. Why like me? I'm no where. I don't exist. She has to be happy. But what if she isn't? If she is crippled by sorrow and is in some asylum or even dead seeing me wander from the heavens and smiling the way she used to with all her innocence . . . I'm going mad . . . Ricky's mind never remained calm.

Reaching home, he ran his eyes through the list of things to be done before the wedding. Cards, event managers, tux, guest list, dance and first . . . . a ring . . . preferably diamond????

No wonder the "I do" stuff is serious. Its cash out and commitment in for the rest of your life. My life?? It's the one wise thing in years to have asked for time to know Jane. What's much to know about her? Well, for sure to buy time I will have to get the ring. Things can wait after the ring but if the ring is late things may seem unsure. What if anyone gets to know about this? Why shouldn't anyone know? I am to marry someday.

Dev was back at Tiara's cottage. She was eagerly waiting at the door to storm him with her questions as usual but Dev wouldn't give in without a coffee and snacks. He did promise some interesting scoop to discuss when on phone with Tiara on his way to her place. For a change Vardhan was home and with Kris and Cherry on the game console. For Dev's smile Tiara's response was spontaneous . . .

"That happens only once in a while. This time it is for Akruti. For a mistake the girl had taken him for brother and the busy body has excused himself for the doted sister at need. I don't remember seeing him after I was out from the hospital with the baby. Had to be with the baby all time, all myself. Nice change this time. This girl . . . has something mystical. I must admit. She could draw hearts towards her. What say Dev?"

"She does . . . that's why I'm here leaving all my work back home. For one person who is nothing but a friend."

She is beautiful for sure gorgeous to the extent any one could die for. But she is so calm and fragile. I wonder what nut the dumbo is to have left her suffer. Look at her even at sleep she's beautiful, an angel in disguise. What would she be dreaming of? Her love? His return? Or what would she be feeling? Pain, peace or fear perhaps. I am a failure to read her mind. Any woman for that case. God himself wouldn't be good enough to read a lady's heart". Dev whispered in Tiara's ear.

Dev left for the kitchen. Tiara had set the environment good enough for discussion. Narration was the best part of Dev and he did add enough masala to the chat to make sure Tiara got stuck to the wooden chair. The scoop seemed to be more than what Tiara could digest.

"For the break it was sure that there were enough cases to crack and the culprit was as said in never land", she summed up.

Dev nodded in approval and sighed . . . leaving the table he tagged "she has to get busy if I have to play the good cop. Get her to work if you can Miss Brainy". He passed a wink that clearly meant a challenge.

Tiara was no bad. Days into the challenge she was all set to buckle the lady back to her seat and for the same she had to pull in Andy and Mandy, the twin trouble. A disastrous pair but they can make the impossible a reality. Glad they were associated with the

Research project and Tiara had to pay a fortune to get the road runners to grope themselves to a boring trail to wisdom they would account to peanuts or even less.

To break the ice she had called for a comeback party for Akruti. All including Damian and Jain who could bring in the grey patches in Akruti's life had been invited. The first round of clearance had passed with Dev.

"Why these guys and what's the twosome doing here? Who are they? I would be rather pleased to know more about your plans Tara. I'm worried it's more than what she can handle." Dev complained.

"The guys you see there were the reason to the breakdown. What ever they had discussed had given her the tremors and the twosome . . . they are just puppets I've hired. They will be associated with Akruti at work and with me off the job. I had a talk with her boss and cleared. They will be more support staff on her work and all stand up comedian if the damsel shall be distressed. I had to pay my purse out to get them into this business and no worries have put them in your account . . . . the mission is to have Akruti surpass these hurdles and with work she will be fine. Hope you get it bro!!" Tiara patted Dev on the back.

The plans had definitely seen a remarkable change in Akruti and she seemed growing out of the trance. The two jesters did their best to relieve her off pressure without leaving a chance to flirt in and out if the office despite of warning notes from all corners. Mandy, the elder twin had a soft spot for Akruti, but wouldn't admit even to his blood half partner. He made sure the latter had a neat conversation unlike with the other feminine lot. He could have expressed his heart out but that wasn't in the agenda and when it came to business sleeping with the clients were off the list and too much to ask for.

Ricky browsed for diamond showrooms in his Black Berry and the mini screen flooded with the names of more than a million outlets of which he could make sure Tiffany were at their best in name and fame. He had heard from some of his own friends cry out the bill they had to bear to appease the desire of their female counterpart.

Finding one in the vicinity he headed to the outlet and being warmly treated he was led to the rings. A large area neatly spread into cubicles where each client was neatly handled by a personalized staff, an expert in the jewel to assist the client. Rather bored after seeing more than a ton varieties of the same stone, he chose a simple ring that carried a huge stone.

"Splendid choice!!! One in a million. The cuts are perfect and purity the best. Can bet this is the most elegant piece we own and could put that in the Victorian collection. Let me help you sir . . . take this towards the day light and experience the quality yourself." the salesman had almost cuffed Ricky to follow him to the large window staring at the road and he obliged.

With the deepest disinterest he followed the instructions to see a million colors on the reflection. Among them her face shown clear and full of life. Distrust had overtaken him. His eyes cheating him for the love his heart held. The mirage was of the lady he loved but the little kids? They must be hers evidently. She's happy and full of life. Time moved and so did the mirage. In no time they had vanished.

"Shall we make the bill?" the salesman broke the spell.

"Yes, send it to my office ", he answered and rushed out.

I can't miss her. She must be here somewhere. She's alive. I will have to meet her. Confess my actions and . . .

In a moment he stood still with a jerk as if his heels had put on a sudden break. What was he going to do? Meet her and apologize. His existence would bring her a shock and what if his existence spoils her happiness and bring her horrid past. Her life would be doomed. Ricky seemed calculating his each step away from Tiffany's.

Being glad that she was alive gave him immense peace. He had trusted he would never meet her again or even declare her dead in his mind.

He hung his head and started walking towards his sedan. His mind still drooled over her. A faint beep caught his attention and the very next moment he was flying off the road towards the light pole. The speed was beyond his control and lo he lay on the pavement with a pool of blood around him.

CHAPTER 21

Love is trust

"Hey you get the sandwiches . . . I've packed them for you." Tiara called out to Akruti. In this short span she had studied her guest pretty well. Mandy was waiting outside the cottage. He had taken up the pick and drop for two reasons. While assisting Akruti with her assignment, they could discuss about their work during the drive and he had developed a layer of over protection towards her. He knew he wanted her. Call it crush or even love but any such hint could spoil his chances to be with Akruti. Being half English, he could very well pair himself with the most attractive feminine folks he'd met.

His 6 foot stature, wild grey eyes and bushy hair that never obeyed him whenever he wanted them to be made neat and the well muscled built he had developed to keep his appearance on the best side drew crowds of women. Perhaps the second half nature being an Indian kept him away or he feared his brother could follow his path made him the eligible bachelor around.

A few affairs, regular quantum of drinks and work kept him happy making sure none exceeded their limit.

Akruti rushed towards the door picking up a pile of files and her snack pack. Tiara would have eaten her raw if she'd left it back on the table. Finding her way out to the porch where the SUV blared the weirdest horn seemed an effort. Her hands were full and her fingers slipped off from the door knob each time she tried to open the door. For the first time she cursed the timing Mandy was home and even the moisturizing crème she held as a resort to face the tough winter there.

A few assignments and Mandy was a reliable coordinator and close aide to Akruti. The reports would be mailed to the office and Andy would do the desk work. Andy, a free spirit found the work allotted more as a stuff to keep him entertained. Mostly occupied in flirting or rugby matches, he kept track of the clients and the assignments they took up. This one with Tiara to assist Akruti was a tricky one. Being together at the University, Tiara had a right to command them. That's fine between friends but this one came as an emergency and was complicated and at the same time delicate as well. Any failure in planning would make the whole plan topple. He trusted his elder brother (by a minute), that he was smart enough to handle the half nut lady.

He had always wondered what would be the reason of the dramatic change in Mandy's life. From day 1 of the client assignment, Andy has seen his brother disturbed or rather distracted. Mandy found company in solitude and had turned to kinda sweet guy. The Rock n roll music had been replaced by romantic hits and the frequent frenzy drive they used to share was converted into long drives with silence despite Andy's frantic efforts to change the mellow drama on wheels.

Envy and rage had whipped his emotions and rage made him blind. But he could easily convert them to pure concern when he realized what ever had been the reason, which made his Mandy happy. He could see himself smile whenever Mandy did. Should admit Andy did envy Mandy for whatever he experienced. His face had such calmness and it turned bloody pink every time he was to go out for the Tiara project. The answer was obvious. There's something Mandy had for the nut lady . . . Akruti. It's not that Andy had vengeance towards her for converting her brother to a bunny but the femme definitely had a spell on his brother.

The day's project was at the child-care division at Sacred Heart Hospital. On the short walk to meet the department in charge to get their seminar on "Child care and Healthy mind" approved, they had to rush themselves across the Casualty, it being the quickest way to the farther end of the block.

On the race, Akruti happened to bump onto the stretcher that whizzed to the OT for surgery. No one had accompanied the injured except the paramedic.

"Immense blood loss. Poor . . . wait I've seen that face . . . . hey he . . ." Akruti couldn't help herself from blabbering. She had no words but the face was so much familiar but before she could be sure of anything Mandy grabbed her tight and took faster strides to the end of the corridor . . .

Mandy clutched her arm tight and accelerated his steps which had converted itself from walking to jogging. On his way he murmured . . . *"What's the matter? You were stuck there. Don't you think we're late to meeting? You seem lost. Are you ok?"*

"I think I know him. His face seems familiar. The guy . . . the one who's at the OT. Can I join you afterwards?" Akruti was perturbed.

Seeing her otherwise pink face flushed off blood, he promised to take her to the Enquiry Section to get the info on the patient. By the time he was out of OT, they would be done with their meeting too.

In an hour they were at the counter to know more about the person injured. *The name was Ricky, a high profile media pro and the case was road accident. There was heavy blood loss and the forms were signed by his wife . . . one Ms. Janet. She will be at the post OT ward. Theirs is a private room. That's all I can tell you. Well, I guess the guy's off danger but can't assure easy recovery. He's got multiple fractures. Might take some time to leave this premises, the* information was good enough for them.

Does it ring any bell? Mandy looked at her eyes

Not sure. But before we leave, I would want to see him. Just to make sure he's fine. Akruti lowered her head in worry.

Knowing that was too much a trouble situation Mandy tried to convince her to leave but seeing her face sink, he took her to the private room and peeped through the window.

The door opened gushing heavy air on Akruti. A lady stood blank before them. She must be in her thirties and in a cracked voice she nearly growled at them.

"What are you guys doing here? This is s private room. Can I help you?"

Mandy had to go through the intro session and the lady seemed to be hooked to her phone and hardly looked at Mandy or Akruti. To his intro, the lady responded that her name was Janet and she was with Ricky, the person injured. All this time Akruti tried herself to get a clear glance of the person. His was injured for sure and his profile was visible. That reminded her of someone dear. Before she could get to the door, Jane patted Akruti's shoulder and as caught red handed in crime she turned in a fraction of second letting her long curls wave in the air.

To her surprise she saw Jane staring at her with her eyes gleaming. Thinking she was a criminal, Akruti confessed that the person inside seemed familiar and just wanted to make sure he was out of danger as the sight of seeing him drenched in blood had disturbed her. Bidding aideu, she hurried herself with Mandy towards the exit leaving the tall woman still staring at her.

"Ok. Project sent to boss . . . I hope alls done. Got to get home before the Power tuffers grab the Blue bonds in the season's match. Ah . . . the messages . . . . 12??? Not bad. Meet me tonight-Cheryl . . . go to hell.

Bills to be paid . . . loan reminder . . ." he tapped with great rhythm on his I-pad.

"Well . . . have to talk meet you at home . . . urgent . . . Andy . . . Now that's crazy." This would have been the very first time Andy has sent a message to Mandy to talk. Guessing the importance, he headed home.

Reaching home, Akruti took herself a place beside Tiara and Dev for tea. The kids were home and that was evident from the noise in the garden.

"Can I get you some coffee?" Tiara asked from behind the counter that separated her from Akruti and Dev.

"I will need some Ti", she fell silent. This would have been the first time Akruti settled for Ti in place of Tiara.

Dev pulled his chair close to Akruti and whispered, *"Kruti what's wrong? Do we need to talk about something?"*

"Dev . . . The girl's upset cos she had met a guy full of blood being taken to the OT and is bit pesky about it. Mandy had called when I was in kitchen." Tiara nudged Dev. She was aware it wasn't as simple as said but an effort to lighten her mood was worthwhile.

Having done with her coffee, Akruti silently retired to her room.

"Now call that a day. She won't turn up for dinner bro, unless you get it sorted. Go fish the mess out of her mind. Psycho doc!". Tiara ordered.

Jane spent her time recalling the face she had seen. It was strongly familiar and had hit her memory.

Yes! The laptop and the cottage. The female is the same one in boss's laptop and his room. Who could she be and how's she here? Does Ricky know she's here? If he knows, he may find her. And where am I then? No . . . She will not remain in his life. Before it's too late, I will have a hand on the girdle. I need Ricky and only I get him.

Love at times play the gruesome game. What is right for one may not necessarily be the same for the other. Keeping her vengeance as sharp as a sword ready for duel, Jane made sure she had enough time with Ricky. She took all the responsibility starting from office to his personal care. What ever it took she was never ready to compromise on her decision.

Sharing her heart with Dev, lightened Akruti. She was sure she had seen Ricky before but the vague profile wasn't enough to confirm any hunch. Dev took up the PI duty assuring he would keep a track of Ricky and convinced her to focus on her assignment and the tour to Dubai in a week's time.

A day before their assignment Akruti took a secret trip to the hospital. She was sure any hint could get Dev, Tiara or even Mandy go mad at her. To her surprise all she could know was that Ricky had been discharged and his female counterpart has taken up all to be with him and take care of him. Knowing there was nothing much left for her to, she had to quit her investigation and prepare for her trip.

Mandy was sure he could get to sit beside Akruti. He had paid more to get the seats despite the non availability. The trip was a chance to be with the lady he had a crush on and to express his wish to be with her.

The trip was long and tiring but he would take any if it is to be with her. Checking into the Hyatt Regency, they retired to their independent rooms with a deal to meet at dinner.

At 9, Mandy was still shaken. Kruti had dragged herself out of bed to call Dev and inform they were fine. With great effort she changed herself to smart casuals, a white crepe shirt and a blue long skirt. She had less or no make up at all. Yet, her face shone bright and her lips juicy pink. Her eyes were sparkling and the thick drowsy eyelids added to the mystique beauty she carried.

She saw Mandy at the bar counter and waved at him. He smiled. As per their plans the assignment could wait for a day or two till they had done enough sight seeing and were ready to concentrate on the assignment. In the 3 week tour 3 days of partying was rightful. Mandy took his drink and took a seat at Akruti's table.

"Hey there . . . How are you? You look sexy today. Party plans??" Mandy giggled.

He seemed odd but Akruti believed the drink had probably brought out his flirtatious nature. She mixed her smile with a comment

"Good. But you seem to be on the higher side. Will you be having something or the drinks will be all?"

"Order for both of us. Anything is fine for me. I could eat an elephant for the hunger I've. Meanwhile lemme get you something to drink. I've heard they have great fruit punch here." he staggered his way to the bar counter.

The food was served and the drink was set. Mandy placed himself comfortable. He was drunk for sure yet the appetite was good. Akruti had her fill and set her hands on the fruit punch. It definitely had a punch but a bit out of normal.

"Perhaps they had some wild fruits here that could give such strong taste to the drink." Akruti felt a bit dizzy. The trip had taken all her energy. She laughed and laughed with no reason. Mandy who was dining opposite to her had nothing to say but smiled. Feeling drained out she tried to return to her room. But her feet were light and had trouble balancing herself on the floor. She clutched Mandy's shoulder and gazed at him.

Her beautiful eyes and wavy hair took away Mandy's breath. He wanted to have her. Strip her right away and got to bed with her. He didn't waste much time and led her to his room. She bid good night but he clutched here tight and kissed her hard. Before she could recognize his tongue had done much in her mouth. He was acting weird and in a jiffy he ripped her sleeve revealing her pale white arm and sleek shoulder.

She pushed him away and slapped him for being rude. With all the energy she had she left the room and found her way to her room and locked it in a jiffy lest the beast should try to tear her into pieces and kill her. She plopped onto her bed and cried. Cried till she never knew she felt asleep.

She couldn't call Dev or even share anything with her mom. This has to be faced and be a secret for ever. A painful secret.

The next morning she woke up the knock at the door. To her shock, it was Mandy all set to breakfast. His face had least botheration of what had happened last night and forget regret. Mandy behaved indifferent towards her and seeing her torn sleeve, he confronted her.

"You promised to meet me at the dinner but never called. I am dead hungry. By the way what's with the torn sleeve . . . I hope the desert and the weather hasn't forced you to strip off yet . . ." Mandy's indifference angered Akruti and she was all set to blast his face off. Before she could make his nose bleed she straight away pushed him out of the room and slammed the door at his face. She yelled from the room what he had done to her and called quits to the project.

Whatever he had heard was never registered in his faint memory. He was asleep all time she was talking about but Akruti wouldn't lie about something like that and her sleeve and the tear on her pale skin proved signs of struggle.

I'm sure I did nothing and would never in dreams try to do such harm to her. Even if it was out of crush or lust. There has been something and I've to find out."

He leaned his hefty body to the door and said nothing but sorry.

"Sorry for everything Akruti. I swear I did nothing purposely. I . . . in fact . . . I'"

Knowing his pleas would be unheard in her agony he left for the reception to clear the bills and vacate the hotel ASAP. From what he had seen Akruti would never want to see him again forget working with him. But all that she said had never been in his wildest dreams or nightmares.

In a flash of second his mind cleared and he was at the reception desk enquiring about the last day's check ins. The info being confidential failed to get him the results. Trying his luck he returned after few minutes and confessed he had forgotten to enter his contact details incase he had to be contacted by his Chief. Sounding earnest, he got his hands on the Register. Wasting no time he ran his eyes through the list of names. Lo at the very end of the page. The address and the name shocked him to core.

"Andy has checked into the hotel? Yesterday evening?? He's been following us?? What the . . ."

In minutes the world seemed reversing itself and everything he heard and saw fell into its place. He rushed to Andy's room just beside his own and barged in. Andy was peering at the swimming pool. More at the women who were having fun in their bright bikini suits.

"You rogue scoundrel. Son of a . . . how dare you lay your filthy hands on her??" Mandy clenched his very own brother's throat until he gasped for air.

"C'mon bro . . . You could have me dead in a minute. And what's about the lady. I was totally lost yesterday and the nut seemed a good one to adorn

my night. She is surely a babe." Andy gave vivid description or everything he would have wanted to do to Akruti all night. Before he could finish he had a killing pain on his face.

"Ouch that hurts! Don't tell me you're hooked to that psycho . . ." Andy yelled.

Mandy could have hurt him more. Knowing his rage would bring trouble, he left the room. Later at noon he called up Akruti using the home phone but she never replied. As the last resort he slipped a note under the door.

Akruti had her stuff packed and waited for the call from the reception. Seeing the note she anticipated Mandy would have slipped the bill to be paid.

The note read:

"Andy has checked into the hotel and he was drunk and high yesterday. I apologize for all the mess he had creted. Though I know everything is irreversible and the whole crap would have deeply hurt you, I promise to do anything and everything that could reduce your suffering. That's the least I could do. I'm sorry and I mean it.-Mandy"

Akruti felt her stomach rumble. She wasn't sure if it was out of hunger or the stress she had been carrying around. She thought about the whole episode and was convinced Mandy couldn't be a beast. She called him on the phone and asked him to wait at the reception.

With his head hung like a dead goose Mandy approached Akruti who had been waiting for him. With not much to talk she walked her way to the restaurant and Mandy followed silently. At the restaurant there was total silence except few clinging sound of spoons or occasional murmers. Amidst the aroma that prevailed Mandy cleared his throat.

"I'm sorry for what happened. But . . . he is my brother and I had to be rude to him. He will be out of the hotel in no time . . ."

Akruti kept a straight face with a blank expression. And before she left groaned she will meet him once the assignment was ready to take off. Somehow her mind seemed to be clogged with too much thoughts. She tried hard to figure out what was going on. The inner call was to disbelieve Mandy as he was the only one who knew she would be at the restaurant and how would have Andy arrived without the knowledge of Mandy.

Dev's call asking her to give a thought over Mandy's proposal to marry her troubled her even more.

"All had to happen now! I am sure I know Ricky. Why does his face disturb me? Mandy had to mishandle his brother for her. Mandy's interested in her. He never hinted anything to her. What was going on in my life?"

Despite her endless confusions, she decided to take things easy and one at a time.

The assignment with the abandoned kids who had been rescued by the Child Home and Peace Foundation in Dubai had been more than they had expected. Cases of troubled minds, orphans and even assaults and disabled came under their review. The purpose of their visit was to study the cases and make a report on the same to send it to the UN Aid for fund allocation and approval to takeover the Institution owing the growth in number of child abuse and abandonment cases.

She had first thought it would be a sweet as butterfly task but there were situations where she had wanted to literally throw up seeing the cases and the suffering. Mandy had been with her throughout all her assignments and the very thought of a visit without him gave her jitters. Putting aside the clout in her mind, she decided to move on and get to know both better. The assignment and Mandy. This was a tough task where she had to keep Rahul out of her mind and life.

Dev had kept himself busy collecting evidences on cases related to Rahul and he had concluded that it would be of minimum priority. Mandy had been decent enough to share his mind with him and he in return had to hint about

Kruti and how she had faced a terrible past. Dev had convinced himself that Mandy and the trip would be a great chance to Akruti to move on with her life for a great future.

As Dev's belief Mandy tried his best to make sure Akruti was fine and did even try his hands on impressing her with gifts and surprises which had a cold response. Andy had vacated the day after mishap. That too without a note of apology or regret. He never called but had definitely sent her a message to be careful and he would meet her on return.

The message to be careful could have been a threat if taken so, for concern from such a rogue was totally uncool.

She had sent a message to Dev saying how she had been indifferent to Mandy. The response said she had to move on if not for her that would be what Dev and Tiara and her whole family wished for.

CHAPTER 22

*L*ove is a war

Back from the tour, the jet lag had taken much of Kruti's time and energy. Her schedule book seemed to be filling up with more issues and meetings with the task of report submission as a topping. For such a job meeting, Kruti found herself into the elevator of Carlton. Knowing she had to find a convincing reason she gushed out at the 18th floor. Far from exiting the elevator, she found herself bang a strong pillar. At the very first site it did look like a pillar but on close observation, it turned out to be a full human form, a man. But the face awestruck Kruti. In return, she could see a pair of fiery eyes glaring at her. The fist that wound her arm and saved a fall now seemed to burn.

In one shove she was placed on the floor. Her eyes were fixed on the six foot figure, she saw black out behind the elevator doors. It was Rahul . . . or like him.

Her lungs seemed to be cotton stuffed and breathing was far unknown for few seconds. With no time to think she got back to her heels and got to the meeting. Concentration was an alien term and she tried to concentrate on each word she faced. Jotting whatever she could, she stepped out with great relief of ending a tormentous experience starting from being late to the elevator, the face and finally she could breathe.

Air filled her lungs once again and she found herself alive. The day had left her famished. Grabbing a hot-dog and lemonade she placed herself on the polished bench at the café. The fountain seemed giving her much pleasure that she seemed endlessly admiring it. Unseen to her were a pair that admired neither the fountain nor the scenic beauty but her.

Ricky sighed. Only if he had let his mind take over, he would have let him be wound to her for ever. For she'd so much in her he could yearn for.

Warm hands squeezed him from hehind. How much he wished it would be her. Jane's voice broke the spell and he slid her hands off him. Much in dismay she wondered what had kept him at the window for so long.

Tell me why I wasn't surprised. That bitch is here and she will take him away from me. I need to do my homework. I know where I've to begin. Jane fumed from within.

Taking a day off, she takes her seat beside Kruti and sparks off her conversation.

"Hey . . . hi there. You are the same person I met at the hospital. Aren't you. To meet Ricky."

Unable to lie spontaneously and admitting Jane had traced her identity, Kruti replied, "Yes, I . . . I . . . it was just confusion I'd. Well, how's Mr. Ricky? Hope he's getting better with his treatment sessions."

"Oh yes he's doing great and is back to work. Have lots of commitments to attend to before our big day. And you are invited for sure. By the way where do you work and on which address should I send you the invite?" Jane blushed.

"Thanks for taking me as a guest though we hardly know each other. I work for a Charitable Society in their research and fund wing. This is my card. You can call me in this number. Got to go before it's too late. Have to do the reports before I get to office. Congrats once again on your wedding."Kruti tried hard to hide her uneasiness and it did reflect quite predominantly.

She took a cab leaving Jane stare at her. She mailed to Dev about what had happened and the similarity Ricky had to Rahul. Hoping this time he wouldn't put her mail under "just forget it" tag, she was home.

Dev was as usual relaxed and all ears to hear Akruti. After a brief discussion of the happenings, Dev was indeed convinced it was time he helped her out. With much evidence ruling out the death of Rahul, he was willing to accept a risk or a chance to do justice to his friend and her hopes.

CHAPTER 23

The proposal

9 am, Cafe Coco Bean

Mandy had ordered his third coffee in an hour. The Kakhis and the light blue sweatshirt gave him a stud look. His blue eyes sparkled every time his mobile phone beeped. He'd tried hard to convince Akruti and impress her. Though the effort yield minimum result, he was happy it did and each time she would message him the updates,he was prompt to reply and reply in the most readable and reachable way making sure his expressions were clear and expected the same. He typed:

Nice to know you are keeping yourself busy. Am stuck in a meeting. Wish you were with me. Will meet you once I am done with this meeting.
Can I take you out for dinner? I mean like date . . . if it doesn't offend you. Awaiting you response,

Madly in love-Mandy.

He smiles at the lady beside him and says he's ready for a talk. Jane confesses her love for Ricky and also explains how the presence of Akruti will disturb her future life.

Jane's eyes widened as she explained, "We seem to sail in the same boat as both of us are unsure about our relationships and if you can chip in your brain and effort we can be on the safer side. Ricky seems to be attracted to Akruti and the lady sees her dead lover in Ricky. I did try to wash her hopes but unless there is some strong winds, the sail seems to get no where."

With a handshake and all smiles, they part their ways.

Akruti reads the message from Mandy to Dev and Tiara. The response is well expected scowl from Tiara. All excited she moaned "Awww . . . how romantic and sensitive. He so much concerned about you. I say you have to go . . . what say Dev?"

Dev patted Kruti gently and whispered "give it a chance and meanwhile let me get to work. I've missed all my sessions. Got to get the messages first."

Dev waited near the door way to drive Kruti to the dinner. His jaws dropped as he saw Kruti walk towards him in the purple evening gown.

The gown had tucked itself to her waist and her figure enhanced giving so much importance to feminity. Her hair was put up in a neat braid and a strand of hair curled itself and settled on her shoulder passing her shiny ear studded in diamond and her pink jawline. He eyes were a sea of emotions that sparkled with no reason and the kaajal added the volume. The long nose shone bright and smooth leading itself to a pair of cherry glossed lips and a dimpled chin.

The necklace clung to her long neck and the gown seemed to unusually highlight her cleavage. The slit gave a peep view at her lean yet silky legs. She looked like the mystic beauty any Urdu poets could have portrayed and the mistress of love.

Dev thought he would be privileged to chauffer her to the dinner even if she had refused his offer to drop her. And he did mention it to her well enough boosting her confidence.

At the restaurant, Dev dropped her and cheered her before he left.

I wish I'd asked Dev to be with me or even cancelled the dinner. It's too late. I've to get through this smoothly. I will . . . . C'mon Kruti, you can do it! She assured herself and pushed the door open.

Finding her way through the dim lighted corridor was a task. She would have preferred a more open area. At the end of the corridor, the waiter led her to the table where Mandy had been waiting for her. He looked stunning in a black suit, hair jelled and pleasant look. He stood at once and took her hand guiding her to the chair and helping her be seated.

His eyes twinkled in the candle light and clearing his throat he murmured,

"You look gorgeous. You always do . . . and I admit I'm in love with you"

Kruti at once gulped the glass of water. The words he had just said especially the second half was way too fast for her.

Not knowing how to respond or rather not willing to respond she kept her eyes low, yet focused on the red candle that gave enough light to see who sat past her and rest of the world seemed to be mere darkness. Her eyes were equally bright as the flame that flickered every time Mandy breathed. He wished she would give him a positive sign. Her silence left him clueless. Collecting all his courage, he spoke up lest he should let the opportunity pass.

"Akruti, I've expressed my feeling for you few times now. Every time I'd wait for a reply and when you remain silent, I convince myself to give you more time to think. I think I have given you enough time to think. I am really in love with you whole heartedly and would love to take you as my wife."

He knelt before her and extended a ring. Before she could pull a word out of her mouth, he popped the question,

"Will you marry me?"

She felt dumbstuck. Here's a guy kneeling amidst of the entire crowd shamelessly and she has to take a decision and reply immediately.

Without much to think, she said "Ok". The least she could do to put away the embarrassment and end the dinner, date . . . whatever. All she wanted to say was "No, I didn't mean it" and neatly leave the restaurant.

He slipped the ring onto her finger and kissed her. Uncalled again and truth that she could feel the kiss turn to a painful mishap. She had been hurt the same way when Andy had kissed her. Though she didn't make a mess of it, there was something conspicuous. With no further words or farewell she headed towards the exit.

Mandy turned to the table diagonally opposite to his and there he saw Jane and Ricky startled. Jane secretly waved at him and Mandy smiled. Ricky held a pale face.

At home Tiara had glued herself to Kruti's bed waiting for her and had dozed off. Kruti made her way quietly to the changing room and was back in her pair of pajama pants and top. Tiara was all set to listen to

Akruti. She wore a pink night dress and had a pillow tucked to her belly to support her elbows that supported the arms that cupped her cheeks as if ready to listen to a fairy tale. In a split second her eyes popped out . . .

"What . . . you are engaged . . . I mean you said yes? He proposed? OMG . . . ." she roared into laughter and turned pink.

Akruti not in mood to bush cursed her memory for not removing the ring before she entered the house and narrated the events at the restaurant.

For few minutes there was silence and Tiara sighed . . . "so you said ok . . . that's not a proper acceptance and you said ok to avoid embarrassment and not because you were ready?"

"Yes, No, Yes, No", Kruti murmured.

"What yes-no-yes-no?" Tiara broke into anger.

Akruti hung her head and placed her head on Tiara's lap which held the pillow.

"Ti . . . I'm confused. It's not that I hate him or don't like him. He's a good guy but I'm not somehow convinced. I don't know how I must explain."

Tiara tried to console Kruti.

"It's just a ring girl. You have time. Wait till you are fully confident about him. Take this as a learning period. Try to know him more and be with each other more so that you get to clear your mind. Meanwhile I'll ask Dev to trace his backgrounds. I mean don't worry, we're there for you.

Ah . . . . your mom had called. Aditi's wedding date is near. She needs to talk to you, so better call her tomorrow . . . first thing in the morning! Good night . . ."

Tiara left the room but the thought of being engaged all of sudden disturbed Kruti. The thoughts kept switching between Mandy and Ricky.

At the parking lot Ricky waited for Mandy and once he turned up, the six foot figure held Mandy by his collar and in hoarse voice mumbled

"How dare you force the ring on her? Let her live. She's mine and I'll slay your throat if I see you near her"

Mandy eased Ricky's hold with a polite smile and offered his hand introducing himself mentioning he had been at the hospital when Ricky was in. Ricky had to get his form back and replied he had not been conscious enough to recognize the faces then.

"Nice day . . . . first you were there at the restaurant and could be a part of my engagement too . . . . the lady in purple. She's my fiancé Akruti. Isn't she gorgeous?" Mandy chuckled.

Ricky felt a clump on his throat. His heart felt heavy and he wanted to bash off Mandy's face that very second. "Yes, she is. Congrats to both of you. So when have you decided to do the knot?"

"Very soon. I can't wait to see her beside me" Mandy shook with excitement.

The very conversation didn't please Ricky and he made a note that this guy was never the best for a woman like Akruti.

But if she is happy, why should I be worried?

Ricky tried to pacify his mind.

The very next morning, Ricky called for a press meet and announced his betrothal to Jane. The news spread like wildfire.

"THE ELIGIBLE BACHELOR AND THE MEDIA BIG BUG TO TAKE THE VOWS SOON WITH HIS ASSISTANT AND CLOSE AIDE JANET"

Dev was the first to get the papers. Seeing the photographs, Dev noticed Ricky's close resemblance to Rahul and read the article which portrayed a brief history of him that dated to a period after Rahul was missing.

This calls for a close investigation. I will meet him today itself. Got to get an appointment with him.

Kruti called her mom. The house seemed to be filled with all sorts of noises. Vessels, laughter, music, chit-chat and even yell. There was so much hustle bustle and she could hardly hear her mom. Waiting for the noise to settle down. Akruti's mom spoke up

"Beta . . . can you hear me? There's so much happening here. Aditi's in-laws had called that the dates had to be day after or else it had to be after a year. So we decided to do it day after itself. I know it's hard but is manageable. Tell me how you are and when are you coming? Mamaji has found few grooms suitable for you. I wish you were here. Aditi would have been happy. Are you eating properly? Dev is there na? Say I need him here soon."

Akruti couldn't hold her tears any further and she broke "Maa . . . how much I miss you all but I can't be there for the wedding the assignment has just started and I'd taken enough days off. Dev is fine and he will be there soon. I won't let him be here for long. Tiara is taking care of me for you maa. Where's Aditi? And do you need cash? I can send you whatever I've ma . . ."

"It's ok beta . . . Kruti take care of your health. Aditi has gone out shopping with Gracy. She is here most of the days. Motherless child. I cook whatever she wishes to have and she is here for you. Does so much lot that you need not worry at all. Mamaji is of great help.

Don't send money. Keep it for your use. I'll ask when required. Please come back soon." mom sniffed.

"Love you maa bye. Will call you later"

Kruti missed all the fun and the love she would have got if she had been at home. But her presence would have definitely triggered a question on Aditi's marriage before hers. Good that she was able to leave. After the conversation, she switched on the television hoping it would divert her thought about home.

The flash news and the main news in all the channels were on Ricky and his engagement. Kruti sat upright and raised to volume high enough to bring Tiara from the kitchen. Both of them glanced at the TV and followed the news. They must have seen repetitions thrice and Tiara turned to see Kruti's eyes like a water-bulb, ready to burst at a brink.

Tiara held tightly to Kruti and whispered "that's Ricky". But beyond her vision Tiara too felt there was something plotted in the Ricky-Rahul fix.

Dev was home at the evening and without further notice, he packed his bags saying he had to be to India in the night flight. Neither neither Tiara nor Kruti asked why. Yet before leaving, Dev confessed that he had met Ricky and latter has denied any info about knowing Kruti.

"Have to take the tougher way around. I will be back in few days and with a big surprise. Sorry I might get married in a couple of days. Will get you all at the party here. Will mail you once I check in. Ti and Kruti keep checking the mails."

Dev bid a quick farewell and fizzed off in the cab that had been waiting for him.

CHAPTER 24

Love is mystery

Friday 6 a.m.

With the winters draping the full stretch of Bay bridge, the wooden structure stood isolated. There was nothing to be seen in the vicinity. Mist had taken the vision to blankness. Perhaps they would be better aware of what was going through Kruti.

She stood all alone in the cold. Her body could feel the piercing pain of the winds but that was nothing to the pain she felt within her. Her cheeks were warm and the lips that went pale white could taste the warm tears that gushed off the large eyes that once showered joy . . .

Why did I even fall in love with him? And why did I have to meet him again? To know he could break my heart each time. To see myself standing with no future and holding on to a life that held no meaning to itself. Forget giving happiness elsewhere, what could I do when I'm not happy myself and when it hurts. And why always me? All I did was love him and love him for my life. My belief and trust. My love brought him back to my life but not for me . . .

Rahul . . . you have betrayed me and left me with nothing. Not even my life or even a future. Nothing but tears and pain. Love never fails but here it did.

Each time she tried to gather herself the flickering images of the press meet and the announcement filled her brain.

Andy emptied the last carton that had nested his game console and cds. He set them below the large screen television. Though he had to pay his pocket out to get the new abode and the interior done to his expectation, he felt relieved. After the chores and cleaning up was done he plushed himself on the couch with a beer. The froth seemed to slide smooth on to his throat and slowly to his hunger stricken palate.

In the second gulp he emptied the bottle followed by a burp that sounded more like a growl. After several futile attempts to place the bottle on the side table, he succeeded letting a photo frame slide onto his lap. Half dozed, he picked up the photograph and smiled. Laughed aloud like a mad man and grumbled at the picture

"You are trapped and he can't help you . . . he is a fool . . ."

He lied on the couch caressing the smooth surface of the picture and soon snored loud.

Dev mailed Kruti from the airport that he had a meeting with Ricky who denied any doubts of being Rahul or even recognizing Kruti.

Though the meeting seemed a waste of time, Dev had other plans which could prove Ricky wasn't a mere resemblance.

CHAPTER 25

The Confrontation

Nagercoil, Tamil Nadu, India

The sea roared it way to the shore sending smooth frothy waves ticking the two pairs of legs. Every time the waves touched, the pair of little brown legs would jump vigorously clumping the sand beneath. The duo walked past the waves to a freshly built thatch roofed block which housed a dozen eye balls curiously peering at the duo approaching them.

The eyes sparkled as they smiled their vision set on the food packets being brought to them.

The man in his early thirties entered the house with a smile patting the shoulder of the tiniest one in the bunch. He them laid a mat neatly on the floor and started opening the food packets. Like swarm of bees attracted to honey the children formed a neat circle around him. He made neat orbs of food and placed them on the palms that stretched towards him. Patience was a word unheard when hunger squeezed in.

The tall fair figure had his share from the same packet making sure the children were full. He then stepped out and walked towards a group of youngsters busy at work. They had plans and blueprints to follow and few sturdy figures to help them.

"How is the work progressing?" he asked.

"The houses shall be ready in a week's time and we will be able to get the families shift here pretty soon." the youngsters replied.

"Good work boys!" he cheered and turned to leave.

"Mandy what would the next project be?" one of the youngsters asked.

"You will know once this gets over!" Mandy replied and winked.

Mandy dragged himself brushing the soft sand. He was a happy man. But he was sure he would have been happier if he would have had his life shared with Akruti. If and if only Andy had not pleaded him to keep himself away from her. Andy's love and desperation for her forced his blood half to leave UK and from his brother's life unnoticed.

Dubai is a cursed chapter to Mandy. As that was the place he met Akruti for the last time and left her to have a peaceful life with Andy as well. His courage waxed away not giving him the courage to disclose his existence in farther corner of the world to anyone he knew.

Mandy let out a huge sigh as he entered his one-room house. Though single room; he made sure he had best facilities to keep his communication networks working.

He dragged a wooden chair and set himself before the laptop to check mails.

Promptly replying to his mails, he came across a wedding invite.

In couple of days, he was at Goa to meet Dev at Anmod.

"Oh fish! Where in the world were you? I couldn't get you on your phone as well." Dev complained.

"Let me in and I will tell you the whole story". Mandy assured.

Mandy spent the evening with Dev narrating his past starting Andy's plea to let him live with Akruti and his decision to visit India for a peaceful cause. He explained the circumstances that forced him to leave Akruti work with Andy in Dubai and henceforth.

"I decided to leave for good and made sure I won't be seen or heard in their lives hence." Mandy hung his head.

Dev sat still trying to chew each word Mandy had uttered. His analysis meters shown danger signals and he jumped from his seat at once.

"You mean you weren't the one with Akruti in Dubai and you never proposed to her? Are you sure?" Dev sounded perturbed.

"Yes. Andy was with Akruti and no I never had the confidence to express my love to her as well." Mandy affirmed.

Dev placed himself heavily on the couch.

"Mandy . . . if it were Andy who was with Kruti why he would not disclose his identity and take your identity instead. I don't feel this good and it definitely gives me awkward vibes. We need to talk and return to UK once the wedding is over. And for you Mandy there's lots to catch up. Will talk over dinner tonight." Dev assured as he led Mandy to the guest room.

In two days, Dev was a married man with a responsible wife and even more to make sure his close companion was saved from any trap set for her. After much deliberation, analysis and pleads, Mandy agreed to join Dev to UK, the place he never wanted to return fearing his past would not allow him to have a future.

Dev pushed the luggage trolley towards the exit followed by Mandy. At the exit they departed ways as Mandy had decided to settle in a motel without having to interfere with Dev's privacy.

Dev headed to Tiara's home and following a brief session on Mandy, he left for the motel where Mandy stayed promising he would meet Kruti once he is sorted with the mess.

Dev hopped into a cab and in few minutes he was joined by Mandy. The drove to Mandy's cottage. Though he had bought it to start his new life with the one he loved, he had to leave it for his brother.

The cab screeched itself to a porch filled with dry bushes and cluttered leaves.

Mandy moved towards the door and knocked. The door was ajar. He entered the living room which seemed more like a pub with uncleared bottles and leftovers.

He tried to find any movement in the house.

With much caution he took the stairs to the bedroom and opened the door. In a second he slammed the door and walked towards the exit.

"Bro . . . hey bro wait up". Andy ran out in his shorts. He clutched Mandy's arm tightly and hugged him.

"Leave me and cut the crap. What in the world were you doing there?" Mandy growled at his brother.

"What? Ohh! That's Claire. We met at the pub. Just a time pass. Nothing serious. You know me right? I can't sleep without company. Soon the nut will take her place!!" Andy chuckled.

Dev, who had been witnessing the drama, clutches Andy's throat and pushes him aside passing a glare at Mandy. He leaves the brothers to fight taking his steps to home.

"That bastard . . . I'm gonna kill him" Andy grumbled.

"I just wanted to know one thing. Is Akruti marrying you thinking you for me?" Mandy confronted.

Andy fumbled and walked back to his cottage. He was pulled back by Mandy's strong hands.

"Answer me or you are dead. I swear!" Mandy retorted.

"Well, I can't say completely. She thinks I am Mandy and I never bothered to correct her. What's in a name? What if I tell her and she goes crazy and backs off from marrying me. I don't get her on my bed or let her know she had messed up with the wrong guy." Andy yelled.

Mandy stood dumbstruck.

"You did this just to take your revenge on her? Knowing that I loved her. I decided to back off just to make sure you are happy. And you just want her to be a toy adorning your bed and pacifying your cravings." Mandy cried.

"Now, stop being a baby Mandy. I told I will marry her. But she will not be the one I spend my whole life with. And why? To be a psycho like her? If you're madly in love with her, you can very well have her after she realizes she has slept with her enemy . . . me. That will make me a winner forever". Andy furiously spilled venom leaving Mandy speechless.

CHAPTER 26

Love is confusing

At Carlton Tower, time's past office hours. Ricky played mind games with the silence he was blessed with. His mind oscillated between Jane and Kruti. He would not want to ruin her life neither would want to be unjust to Jane who has accepted to share her life with him despite all his limitations.

His silence was invaded by foot steps that neared his cabin. But he never bothered to give heed to the change in his status quo.

The door creaked open. He remained calm. His mind was convinced there was nothing that could break his peace. Silence echoed and in it the mild scent of feminine perfume soothed his senses. Judging Jane was back at office, he grumbled "Not now Jane. Let me be to myself."

There was no reply. Ricky turned to the lady seated before him. His shock forced him to jump from his seat and he shivered not knowing how he had to react. His reflex has frozen giving him no clue to act.

"You didn't expect me here. Right Mr. Ricky? You wouldn't know me either. Right?"

"I wonder what forced you to be surprised or rather be shocked seeing me", she shot one question after another to the man who until now had command over himself and many more around him.

"I . . . you . . . how come you and how did you . . ." Ricky baffled.

She left the cabin and he followed her like a mad man.

"Wait . . . listen to me. Sruthy please listen to me" Ricky scowled.

"Thank God . . . you remember my name bhai. Your new identity had gifted you forgetfulness as well I understand and the same would have erased everything that could remind you my existence as well." She retorted.

Dev held Ricky from behind.

"So . . . well Mr. Ricky. Sruthy is your sister as well? I thought she had just one brother, Rahul." Dev's words had struck the right person at the right place. Ricky remained silent.

Ricky had lost it. He was no longer able to hide himself. His affection for his sister had failed to keep his identity intact.

Words failed when emotions overtook the siblings.

An hour into the meeting, Dev took control of the situation.

"So what forced you to take such a step by hurting everyone who loved you?" Dev was curious.

"My face would have answered half of your question and why I'd to deceive those who loved me . . . well I lost myself and my mind never wished to hurt the so called loved ones and I had no courage to look back into my past." Ricky broke into tears.

Dev broke into fits of laughter which angered Sruthy.

"Bhai you decided to disown us for this silly reason and thought we were not worth a second chance to have you in our lives? Forget us. Even Kruti??? What harm did she mean to you? You would never realize what all she had to go through just because of this stupid reason which you have put before us. I swear I don't take this as a valid explanation. That too for leaving a woman you loved to be half dead and half insane." Sruthy yelled furiously.

"I know what I had done was not right and any explanation I give would never compensate for the loss I had created".

Ricky rested his heavy body on his hands taking support of the table.

Sruthy walked towards her brother and rested her head on his shoulder.

"What has happened is a past bhai. There's still time to correct everything. We had missed you a lot. But you can change everything bhai. If you wish." Sruthy held tightly to her brother.

"No. No Sruthy . . . it's too late for a comeback. I have no right to any happiness. All I am left with is my scarred face and my memories. I don't deserve love or any such emotions in my life." Ricky confessed.

"Let's leave it for now. Better get us home before we are stuck in your office". Dev said as he tried to relive the pressure.

They talked all the way till they had reached Kruthi's home. Before she got off the car, Sruthy looked at her brother one last time.

"Can you give a life to Kruthi? She loved you bhai . . . and loved you so much that she lost her life in wait for you. She had decided to marry Mandy not with heart but as a mere adjustment to try to convince herself that she has moved on. But I know bhai she hasn't. She will not be happy with anyone other than you . . ."

"I have given my word to Jane. I cannot break her heart. I will meet you tomorrow. Will call you and confirm the location." Ricky sighed as he screeched the vehicle off to the road.

At Tiara's home, festivities had just begun. Kruthi spent her time mostly with Sruthy who found it pretty hard to hide the fact she had been with Rahul all evening.

"Sruthy . . . is there anything you are hiding from me?" Kruthi peered at Sruthy.

"Na . . . bhaabhi . . . nothing" she replied.

Despite her assurance, Kruthi was not convinced about Sruthy's answer and was sure the lady had something fuming in her mind.

CHAPTER 27

You reap what you sow

The next morning, Dev leaves home to meet Ricky. They meet and on their way ahead they pick Mandy.

The well protected concrete building gives way to their vehicle through the well guarded wrought iron gates.

They leave the car and enter the office which was blank and well lit. The walls indicated no signs of life and the existence of any human form came into notice only after they neared the office of the sergeant.

Mandy handed over a set of documents to the officer who scanned the trio head to toe. He then took them to a large room with barbed window just adequate to see a face.

Minutes into their wait, a face appeared on the window. Ricky was astonished by the resemblance it had to Mandy who stood beside him. Mandy walked towards the window with Dev.

"If only you had not been so cruel to Kruthi . . . now it's your turn to enjoy your life here." Mandy said and left the room. Ricky joined Dev as they followed Mandy.

"What did Mandy say about him and Kruthi? What happened to her?" Ricky confronted Dev.

"I would have told you if you were Rahul." Dev smiled.

Ricky took the poke as a penalty and rushed out with Dev. After much persuasion, Dev rewound the events from the day he had met Kruthi and what forced her to get married to Mandy. He also confessed that Andy was never the best suit for Kruthi who had decided to try her luck betting her life at stake.

Ricky felt restless as he drove the men back to their destinations. He left for his cottage and spent the day thinking what Kruthi had been through. Guilt ate him from within. He had let her suffer and hurt her.

How could he ever heal the wounds he had gifted her? How would he face her to tell her the truth which forced him to hide his identity? How would he explain his situation to Jane who had by now started dreaming of a life with him? How many lives more is he going to ruin?

Questions were unanswered and he was sure they would never be as well.

CHAPTER 28

Band baaja baraat—the wedding

The day broke with sound of laughter and music which filled the air. The scent of fresh flowers and incense added to the beauty of the morning. There were giggles of joy and tinkle of anklets. Male presence seemed to be minimum at the Rai's residence which was fully thronged with women.

A sneak peek at the interiors gave a clear picture of what was happening there. Women adorned in all colour outfits and sparkling jewellery. They were seated neatly in a row around a young lady who turned pink each time she was teased by her friends and relatives.

Music gave way to frequent outbreak of dance steps from the audience. The lady who had been sitting in the centre chirped as handfuls of turmeric was been applied to her arms, face and legs.

She glowed for sure. Could it be the turmeric that worked oh her skin that gave her the glow or was it the joy of getting married to the one she loved that enhanced her charm?

The fun and frolic extended itself to the evening and the venue had transformed itself to a party hall. Huge floral decorations found its place on the wall and the color was red. The music too had changed from traditional beats to fast Bollowood hits jamming the street.

The young lady now had adorned a heavily brocaded Sari and she was jewel studded as well. She smiled occasionally and the handsome young man beside her winked at her every now and then to which she responded with a pat on his lap.

Her hands were decorated with Mehendi as well. Starting from her fore arm to her finger tips. She proudly displayed the art work on her hands to the photographers who constantly let their flashes work on the couple capturing their finest moments for a life time.

They were greeted and blessed by the old and young equally. In few hours the couple was led to a decorated *Mandap* to do the nuptial rituals which would bind them in a life long relationship coated with love and strengthened with trust.

She sits beside her groom as the priest chanted the mantras. She was perhaps the happiest person in the world. What were her eyes searching for amidst the crowd? Is she awaiting someone special? As the mantras were nearing its end, her heart beat faster. Soon the sound of her heart beat was able to blanket any other sounds around. She trembled. Happiness was evident from her smile yet she trembled. Every cell in her body shook vigorously. The fear of leaving her home for years since birth was too much to take. But keeping all memories safe in the depths of her heart she had to move on. Life demands this from any woman. God has given this strength only to women to be a princess at their home and leave everything to make a new home her heaven. She is the only one holding the courage to pierce her heart and leave her home to bring joy to somebody else's home.

The circumambulation was over and her forehead adorned the holy vermillion sanctifying her relationship for a life time.

The crowd dispersed into smaller groups as they moved towards the fooderia to pacify the palate. Starting from Samosas to Paneer Koftas there were varieties of delicacies; representing the whole nation on a circular plate each guest held.

Almost an hour into the feasting, loud music broke the trend and the beats started forcing the hoggers to sway and tap to the rhythm.

It started with disco and moved on to Punjabi hits.

The groom's parents broke the ritual and got into groove followed by their son.

Her college team, she mingled with had their dance shoes ready as well and they had made up their mind to hold this occasion as a reunion. A well thought out plan which was displayed with precision. They had worked towards making this day a memorable gift to her, the bride.

She could see Happy Singh happily jumping to the tunes. He looked more like a large ping pong ball forced on the ground. Gurmeet Aunty, Happy's wife didn't bother to stop her inflow of delicacies for the entertainment.

Lucky and Jackson, also kids of her colleague, who until now let out burps of Coke, set aside their refreshments and added glamour to the stage. They chased each other and made sure they were omni present having their faces evident in all the snaps clicked.

Maniben smiled as the pie topping found place on her cheeks and around her lips. Though she had been just a helper at their home, her efforts had been worth a note. She deserved more pies for her hard work.

Julie aunty was busy boasting about the Ladies Club elections she organized and to add she displayed her array of diamond accessories attracting women crowd. While Ramdev Chachu and Lalitha Chachi had their share of romance in the corner of the garden. They had found a warm and lonely space for them to enjoy the show and have their privacy undisturbed. Must admit very few couple cherish their love even in sixties. They were a perfect pair to her like bread and butter or let us put it like honey and honey bee . . . or better leave it to them to decide.

Few men, young and old found solace in the hot drinks counter which kept them warm while the fogs arrived to accompany the night.

She saw her mother happy and well treated by the crowd. A crowning victory for wonderfully organizing the wedding and keeping her chin up despite all lows she had faced in life.

Little Nina and Nitika of her neighborhood found joy in bursting the balloons which indicated it was high time they were put to bed. Their crankiness took to bursting the balloons.

Not to be left out was the lady with a baby bump, now far huge than a baby bump. She more or less resembled an air balloon. The lady at the corner table waving her hand at the bride and tapping her toes to the music . . . Gracy, a friend and more a sister.

She danced too with her man. Few funky steps bringing the event to a close. She wished if her Kruti was there. The charm and presence at the wedding would have been fairy tales come true.

CHAPTER 29

Love is complicated

Dev sipped his cup of coffee and in a brink, set it back on the table sticking out his tongue.

"It's burning hot!" He complained as Tiara and Sruthy set the breakfast table.

"I don't remember you asking for a cup of Cold Coffee!!" Tiara nudged Sruthy as she responded to the complaint.

Dev kept mum and smiled. He was sure he could never be a match to the lady's word war.

At breakfast, the arena sounded full of discussion and debate which fell silent as Akruti entered. She innocently passed a glance at all the faces and seated herself in a quiet corner of the table.

The was no word exchange or eye contacts except for some glances at each other.

Sensing the unsurety about the time of her entry for breakfast, she ended her breakfast with a glass of juice and an apple and quietly left the room.

Akruti kept herself busy with her project reports and diary notes in her room where her level of comfort had developed giving her immense security and peace.

Soon, Dev and Sruthy entered breaking her solitude. They found conversation to be something new and difficult to accomplish and Kruti had to break her silence to bring the room into life.

"Now tell me what's that you wish to discuss and what in the world is dragging you guys back from talking to me?

Have I ever been a stranger for you both to think so much to talk about anything? And any crap thing for that matter?" Kruti fired her frustration.

She had been bugged lately with the way Dev and Sruthy behaved once they had tied the knot. They seemed to be less familiar and more strangers to her.

Dev peered at Sruthy to which she responded with a slight nod.

"Well, it's nothing Kruti we were just in doubt whether we have to discuss past issues when you have already decided to move on with your future. But the same, if not discussed should not trouble you in future. This was the stuff which put us in dilemma."Dev confessed.

"Which past and what about future? I wish we could be the way we used to be avoiding these prologue and paragraphs" she whined.

"It's about Rahul and his resemblance to Ricky." Dev continued without leaving a chance to have an eye contact with Kruti; lest her reaction stop him from disclosing the truth.

"I did do some background work with Ricky's past and after much investigation put a conclusion that Ricky was indeed Rahul. But it was strongly denied by him and I had to put an end to my detective gene."

"I know you have taken much trouble for me. Perhaps, it's just an awful misunderstanding or a silly confusion Dev. It's better we leave it." Kruti consoled

Dev as she patted his shoulder and walked past him to the book shelf.

"That's what I thought but it's not true." Dev shot back.

"I decided to get married in a jiffy and brought Sruthy here just to make sure my hunch was not wrong and it paid."

"What do you mean by it paid?" Kruti broke the flow.

Sruthy walked to Akruti and held her tight.

"Bhaiyya is back. He is alive and you knew he would be right, bhaabhi?" Sruthy clung on to Akruti as she sobbed.

"Ricky is indeed Rahul and he couldn't hide himself before Sruthy. We had no plans to let him to either." Dev affirmed.

Akruti sank into deep silence.

"But why Dev? Why me? Why did he do this to me? What had I done to him for which he decided to disown me and distrust my feelings for him?" Kruti's eyes overflowed.

Dev explained what had happened and what had kept Rahul from returning to his life after the accident he had. He made it a point to keep the reasons balanced to allow Kruti to have her say on what she had heard.

Kruti remained unshaken.

She kept herself calm as she kept her eyes fixed on the backyard garden.

"Perhaps you are right Dev. It was a mistake talking about past when I had decided to move on with my future. Perhaps he disowned me because he trusted just himself and not we had felt for each other. He believed

I had fallen for his looks and not his soul. That is too much to take from a man you love.

Perhaps, I'm not the right match for him or may be he's not worth my love at all." She flexed her grip on the window and walked out of the room.

Dev had no words to stop her and he looked at Sruthy for help. Sruthy remained silent as well.

By evening, the house felt more like it was mourning someone's loss.

Tiara, Dev and Sruthy had found their respective places at the tea table.

"So . . . things are not good as we thought it would be huh?" Tiara popped.

"I'm happy it ended this way." Sruthy replied which invited stares from Dev and Tiara.

"When I talked to bhai last time we met, he was quite sure in his decision to move on with his life and confessed he wouldn't want to break up his relation with Jane at this point of time after giving her hopes. He seemed disturbed by his jeopardy but stern in his plans for sure. I feel what has happened is for good. If Akruti had wanted to relive her past, she would have felt miserable by the way bhai had responded to my request to come back to our lives." Sruthy confided her worry.

"I am not going back to a man who has broken my heart and distrusted my love for him. This will be the end to any discussion on my past. It high time all of us move on rather than being treated like fools following a mirage."

Kruti tormented as approached the trio.

"By the way, I am taking a short break and getting back to mom. Had not been at Aditi's wedding too. Will keep you guys updated once I reach there. Do inform

Mandy as well if he enquires. Or . . . . just inform him I need time to decide.

Dev, can you get me to the airport tomorrow? I have done my bookings online. Hope you guys would join me in few days or it's alright. I don't want to bother anyone for anything at all anymore. Have had enough of everything."

Akruti was calm. And her words concrete. She had made her mind strong. The decision not to return to or let Rahul be a part of her anymore had shook her life but she was never a loser. If she could bear his loss in these years, she has learnt to survive and she will too. But what with her future and her mom? She would never allow Akruti to remain unmarried. Akruti will have to give up her might and give in to her mom's decision. Marriage will happen. May it be with Mandy or with someone Mamaji finds suit for her.

She was sure what was kept in store for her future but it would be a million times easier to live than the pain and deceit the man she loved and waited for all this time had given.

CHAPTER 30

Love is divine

Two years later, Bengaluru

Akruti felt a warm hand wind around her. It caressed her arm and stretched itself over her hip scooping her small but noticeable bump in the place of her stomach. A bounce from within brought a gentle smile on her face. A smile which had taken his breath away and still captivated him. A smile which she lost not once but many a times which took him years to return.

He kissed her ear and hugged her tight.

"Relax, I'm not leaving. I'm too tired to leave." She whispered her eyes still shut.

"I'm still scared. You left me once and promised never to return.

If only I hadn't reached on time, I would have missed you forever. You wouldn't have listened to what I had to say or would you?" he said softly.

"I'm sure I would have gone. Gone for good . . . and in none of the movies the heroine returns when she's been asked to by the hero. I'm nothing less." She sighed as she turned towards him and rested her head on his chest.

"But I still wonder you could have been with a hero rather than a villain who ruined your life. If only this Andy-Mandy confusion had not disturbed you. I still feel this face troubles you and all I pray is that whatever happens you should not hate me for what I had done to you and to others." He ran his fingers through her curls.

His heart seemed to beat faster and Akruti could feel his warm tears on her forehead.

She ran her fingers gently over his face and raised her head.

"I fell in love with you not once or twice. But more than a hundred times and it is not the face I fell in love with. These eyes which to me shone like a sea with deep secrets within. That forced me to love you. I had decided not to share my life with anyone but your love forced me to rethink. These scars aren't deeper than the loss I would have faced without you in my life."

She smiled as her eyes burnt. She forced her eyes open but the she felt her eye lids weighed more than her force and they fell shut. She felt her stomach which seemed as if the protrusion had vanished. She jumped from her bed and ran towards the mirror. She was no longer pregnant.

With much despair she rested her body on the bed thinking how many years more will the dreams she had wished to be true haunt her.

In an hour, she had swiftly floated through her routine duties and was on her way to the bus bay. Before she left, she placed a bunch of red roses and placed them dearly before a portrait which reflected the face of her love and life—Rahul.

"Good morning . . . I won't leave you as I promised. You lost your will and left us. I miss you and love you!" she said as her eyes turned red and throat choked.

This was the last step of her morning duties before she left for work. Silently, she crept to the bedroom and had one last look at the mirror. She smiled as she touched the scar on her forehead. A parting gift from her love before he left her.

At his death bed, he murmured to her "I love you but I will not survive. If I do I'm as good as dead. Allow me to leave and promise me you will not fail me but shattering your life and making no meaning out of it. You are a special woman, a great lover; a wonderful wife. You will be a funny mom as well." He said with a smile that vanished as pain dominated.

She remained silent holding on to his arm.

"You can't do this to me Rahul. Not this time. Not now when I need you the most. We need you. Our baby needs you." She whispered hiding her grief.

"Hang on sweetheart . . . Be brave." He held tightly to her arm and breathed his life out.

That one minute of distraction had cost her life. If only he had been cautious. Less adventurous, he could have been with her. She breathed heavily and turned around. Leaning to the cradle, she picked up the tiny soul which lay peacefully unaware what she had lost and what she had left with her.

Kruti carried little Arav and put him gently on her bosom. She walked to the bus bay and boarded X-14.In few minutes she was at her destination.

He waited for her at the bus bay and walked together to the 'House of Children', a dream started by Rahul, nurtured by her and now supported by him.

"Same dream I guess. You are a great woman Kruti. You shall live past all dreams to realize dreams of many needy children out there at our home." Mandy walked beside her as he held her by her shoulder.

They are friend or may be more than friends who shared lives, interest and dreams. Arav was his best friend or a son. They lived their life with each other, supporting each other though they never lived together. In Arav she saw her Rahul, his eyes which took her to a mystical world and still does each time she looks at the tiny face with a smile that mesmerizes her.

Mandy loved her and wished to marry her but as a reply his proposal, she would just smile. The way she always did.

She couldn't and wouldn't let go Rahul.

Rahul taught her to love, to dream, to hope, to wait, to hate, to forget, to live life—Akruti style. He taught her how to live past defeats and walk past falls and gifted her memories she could cherish lifelong. Above all, he gave her Arav-the meaning to her life, the medicine to her wounds and the source to her existence. She learnt to live from him. She learnt to love through him. Rahul . . . her book of love.

She believed life is a puppet show which would go on until the master puppeteer decides to cuts the strings.

This is life Akruti style . . . this is love Akruti style!

Who knows what the great master puppeteer has kept in store for them?